"Hilarity and motherhood, marriage and grace become a teetering foursome in Kim Stuart's humorous first novel. *Balancing Act* is the story I'd attempt to write if I were a young mom — it's quirky, thoughtful, and comically entertaining!"

—RAY BLACKSTON, author of *Flabbergasted*

"Kimberly Stuart has masterfully described the busy world of a new mother with fresh detail and surprising hilarity. Prose is her art, and her fresh wit makes Heidi Elliott a joy to get to know."

—JENNIFER RUISCH, author of *Faith and the City*

"I love Kim Stuart's *Balancing Act* — it is a literary work of genius! Few authors describe motherhood with such rare authenticity and laugh-out-loud candor. And she doesn't pull any punches for the reader dealing with trappings that unguarded marriages can fall prey to. Well done! I can't wait to read the next Heidi Elliott novel!"

—BARBARA ROSBERG, cohost with Dr. Gary Rosberg
of the nationally syndicated radio show
America's Family Coaches LIVE; coauthor of
Divorce-Proof Your Marriage

D0096332

Kimberly Stuart

NAVPRESS®

BRINGING TRUTH TO LIFE

OUR GUARANTEE TO YOU

We believe so strongly in the message of our books that we are making this quality guarantee to you. If for any reason you are disappointed with the content of this book, return the title page to us with your name and address and we will refund to you the list price of the book. To help us serve you better, please briefly describe why you were disappointed. Mail your refund request to: NavPress, P.O. Box 35002, Colorado Springs, CO 80935.

NavPress
P.O. Box 35001
Colorado Springs, Colorado 80935

© 2006 by Kimberly Ann Ruisch Welge

All rights reserved. No part of this publication may be reproduced in any form without written permission from NavPress, P.O. Box 35001, Colorado Springs, CO 80935.
www.navpress.com

NAVPRESS, BRINGING TRUTH TO LIFE, and the NAVPRESS logo are registered trademarks of NavPress. Absence of * in connection with marks of NavPress or other parties does not indicate an absence of registration of those marks.

ISBN 1-60006-076-5

Cover design by The DesignWorks Group, Tim Green
Cover photo of woman by Getty Images, Max Oppenheim
Cover photo of baby by PhotoDisc
Author photo by Mindy Myers

Creative Team: Jeff Gerke, Kathy Mosier, Arvid Wallen, Bob Bubnis

This novel is a work of fiction. Names, characters, places, and incidents are either the product of the author's imagination or are used fictitiously. Any resemblance to actual events, locales, organizations, or persons, living or dead, is entirely coincidental and beyond the intent of either the author or publisher.

All Scripture quotations in this publication are taken from *THE MESSAGE* (MSG). Copyright © 1993, 1994, 1995, 1996, 2000, 2001, 2002. Used by permission of NavPress Publishing Group.

Stuart, Kimberly, 1975-
    Balancing act : a Heidi Elliott novel / Kimberly Stuart.
    p. cm.
    ISBN 1-60006-076-5
    1. Working mothers — Fiction. 2. Family — Fiction. 3. High school teachers — Fiction. I. Title.
PS3619.T832B35 2006
    813'.6 — dc22
2006015732

Printed in the United States of America

1 2 3 4 5 6 7 8 9 10 / 10 09 08 07 06

FOR A FREE CATALOG OF NAVPRESS BOOKS & BIBLE STUDIES,
CALL 1-800-366-7788 (USA) OR 1-800-839-4769

To Edna Mae Roggen,
Wilma Marie Ruisch, and Patti Sue Ruisch,
on whose tall shoulders I stand.

Psalm 90:1

acknowledgments

I am grateful to . . .

... The God of grace, who is inordinately creative in how He lets me love Him back.

... My rock-star parents, Randy and Patti Ruisch, for their stubborn belief that my A- in Freshman English (1989) was not the pinnacle of my literary career. My love for God grows out of theirs, and I am thankful for this most precious gift.

... My brother, Ryan, for loving me even though I made him play "library" when we were little, and to his illustrious writer wife, Jennifer, who fed her sick addiction to editing through all stages of this book.

... My little sister, Lindsay, who is blind to my faults and wide-eyed in her loyalty. She amazes me with her infectious joy, her storytelling prowess, and her profound compassion.

... The extended Ruisch and Roggen families for loving me right through my inability-to-share-my-toys stage, my use-the-Bible-as-a-weapon stage, my angst-filled-poetry-writing stage, and many more that will remain within the family, *won't they*?

... Barry and Jocelyn Welge for their diligence and care in raising the man who lives up to his hero status in our house.

... Scott Welge, who faithfully reminded me that I could expect God to finish what He started.

… Ryan, Betsy, and Olivia Beach, who know how to *really* live and give me the pleasure of shimmying through right along with them.

… Tracey Orman for coming to my rescue a second time around.

… Chef Robert Lewis for laughter that risks asphyxiation and for the inspiration behind Willow's Pasta of Love.

… Sherry and John Swanson for excelling in their roles as Irrationally Biased Cheerleaders.

… Amy De Boef, Amy Hanson, Holly Van Kirk, and Kristen Smith for their friendship, laughter, and quick comfort when my life is reduced to sleep schedules and bowel movements.

… Suzanne Ohlmann for her head, her heart, and her extensive knowledge of synthetic foods.

… Rachel Maassen for loving me since infancy and then bringing my children safely into their own.

… The Rutz family, who taught me courage.

… The original Moms' Group at Hope Church, who didn't flinch at the ranting lunatic from Iowa.

… The quintessential Southern gentleman, Ray Blackston, for looking past the rough draft and whose commitment to the craft of writing is surpassed only by his kindness to this Yankee novice.

… Andrea Christian, who set the whirlwind into motion but not without taking the time to offer me her friendship as well.

… My editor, Jeff Gerke, for taking a chance, trimming the flab, and for not being a telemarketer.

My children, Ana Kiersten and Mitchell Caleb, are even more glamorous to me than landing a book contract. I ache with my love for them and thank them for being the real protagonists.

Finally, I am most grateful to my husband, Marc, who put up with chaos, an overabundance of takeout, and a muttering, pajamas-clad wife, all for the sake of a crazy dream. To this man, who can pull off show-stopping pyrotechnics in the heart of a Dutch girl, I give my thanks and all my love.

prologue

Despite the fact that women had done it for centuries, the whole experience nearly killed me. In my weakest moments, I'd recall with shame the *National Geographic* images: a peasant in the African bush doing it alone, or a teenage bride squatting on the floor of the Amazon, still able to stir the tribe's evening meal with her free hand. I, of course, was pampered and Western. I'd been sanitized, sanctified, and stitched, all in a "birth suite" at St. John's Hospital. The nurses even brought me a steak dinner to celebrate.

Even so, I still came close to a nervous breakdown in the chaotic months following the steak and the stitches. Perhaps by writing it all down for you, I'll make a bit more sense of it for myself. Maybe I'll even dare renew my subscription to *National Geographic*.

chapter/one

"Now, I need you to focus," I said, screwing up my face in concentration. "The black or the stripes?"

My conspirator fixed me with a blank stare, blue eyes unblinking.

"Need more information? Okay. Choice Number One: classic black suit, complete with a jacket that covers expanded girth and breasts suddenly, alarmingly voluptuous."

No response.

"Right. Choice Number Two: a bit more daring with a pink angora sweater, the must-have this fall, but still comfortable with flared charcoal pants."

"Argstf. Moolrsh?"

I paused to consider the counsel, then, "I agree. I'm going black." I leaned over to kiss my six-month-old daughter, Nora, on her cheek. "Thanks for your help, fashionista."

Perhaps I should have been concerned about seeking and following the advice of a girl wearing footie pajamas, a bib, and three quarts of saliva, but I had precious little time to dwell on that. I was on my way to meet grown-ups, people.

Nora watched me from her perch on our wrought-iron queen bed. Her red striped pajamas were distant cousins to our comforter, its narrow lines woven in three shades of green. The wall behind Nora was painted the most vibrant shade of the three and made my daughter's eyes sparkle a deep Dutch blue. Her chubby frame was propped to a sitting position with the help of two pillows. "Gyeoroish," she said, gnawing with gusto on the handle of a toothbrush.

"I know, sweet pea, I'll miss you, too. But you're going to have a great time with Lauren." I stuffed my lactating bosom into a black bra I'd bought in late pregnancy. The end result reminded me of a tourniquet. I pulled on my pants, taking care not to slice any stretch marks with the zipper, and donned my suit jacket. When I looked back at Nora, she was falling onto her side in slow motion like a timbered tree, grinning the whole way down.

"Need some help, lovey?" I picked her up under the armpits, burrowing kisses into the neck I knew had to be somewhere underneath those jowls. Nora smelled of lavender baby soap and puke, equal parts. I slung her and her soggy toothbrush onto my hip and made my way to the bathroom to check our reflection in the mirror.

Frazzled twenty-nine-year-old female flanked by wide-eyed, gurgling infant intent on oral hygiene.

Brilliant. Let the games begin.

ℰ ℈ ℰ

"So, I think that's everything."

Lauren the Wonder Babysitter looked at me with huge, fifteen-year-old doe eyes. I knew her family from church and

had asked her a few times before to stay with Nora. Lauren
was homeschooled and conscientious, like Aunt Bea inhabit-
ing the body of Hillary Duff. "We'll be *fine*, Mrs. Elliott. Not
to worry."

Adolescent babysitter or cruise ship hostess? "My cell
number is on the fridge, in case you need anything. I won't be
more than a few hours."

"Sounds good."

Nora was already engrossed in the educational toys Lauren
had brought along, each of them appropriately challenging
but not overstimulating.

Seriously.

"All right, then. I love you, sweetheart." I smooched Nora
five times on cheeks, forehead, and various other fleshy places.
She didn't notice, fully content on Lauren's lap. "Have a good
time, um, learning. Thanks, Lauren."

Aunt Bea flashed me a golden-girl smile. "Enjoy!"

Wow.

e ා e

I started up the Beast, my term of endearment for my '87
Civic. No matter what you read in the papers, teachers do not
roll in the wealth of your squandered tax dollars. The Beast, in
all its chipped maroon glory, was coughing, sputtering proof.

I revved 'er up and pulled onto Winwood Lane, stew-
ing over Lauren's amazing confidence around children. Six
months ago, of course, a Wonder Girl babysitter would not
have evoked any reaction in me, much less the furrowed-brow
one I felt now as I merged into morning traffic. Why did it

matter one whit that Lauren-for-President commandeered my household better than I did? Why did I feel like a bumbling fool who didn't know formula from engine oil?

Where was the Heidi Elliott of yesteryear? Summa cum laude graduate of a prestigious university. Master's degree in education. Career woman, community volunteer, devoted wife and friend. Now reduced to a complete pansy in the presence of an abnormally maternal fifteen-year-old pixie.

My black suit and I were on our way to rejoin the workforce. After having Nora, I had taken a semester's maternity leave from my position as a high school teacher. The fall term was swiftly drawing to a close, and I was on my way to meet with the principal and my long-term substitute to iron out the details of my return after Christmas.

I'm ready, I assured myself as I slapped on lipstick and powder found under a crusty burping cloth at the bottom of my purse. I puckered up, checking my reflection in the rearview mirror as I drove.

"Whole stretches of hours without Elmo, for example," I said aloud. I couldn't help but grin at my own face, barely able to place a time when I could walk anywhere in a building without clutching a baby monitor.

I might even try urinating with the door closed. Maybe eat lunch, brush my teeth before noon. . . .

The shrill ring of my cell phone startled me out of reverie. Was Lauren crumbling under the pressure? "Hello?"

No such luck. It was Jake.

"Hi, honey. Are you on your way to school?" asked my husband of five years over the background hum of the paint store he owned and managed.

"Yep. I'm almost there. I'm a bit nervous but doing my best to conjure up feelings of *I am woman, hear me roar*. Do you?"

"Do I what?"

"Want to hear me roar?"

"Sure, but how about after we light some candles and put on a little Barry White?"

Astounding how deftly they can work that in, isn't it?

"Okay, Barry, I'm at the school now, so I'll have to coach you on the finer points of marital bliss later. Thanks for checking up on me."

"Break a leg, babe. You'll rock their bulletin-board world." He lowered his voice. "Give my best to the Iron Maiden."

"I'll give her a peck on the cheek just from you." I heard Jake snort. "See you tonight."

I put my phone on vibrate, tossed it into my purse, and got out of the car. Before me loomed Springdale High School, the bastion of higher learning at which I had been professionally fulfilled and grossly underpaid for half a decade. Function had conquered beauty in the architectural battle for the high school: The building was long and rectangular, an extended blur of gray brick with black trim. Three tiers of flags in front offered the only point of visual interest, at least until you met the student body.

Crisp November air greeted me, catapulting me into the world of sharp pencils, blue-lined notebook paper, and Friday football games. I headed past the flagpole toward the double doors and thought, It's good to be back.

℮ ℈ ℮

"Well, look who's here." Dorothy McMinn looked at me over her glasses. She sat sentry with impeccable posture, manicured hands folded neatly in front of her cardigan. Springdale High School's secretary for thirty-six years, Iron Maiden McMinn was an even mix of severe German nurse and a pit bull that fancied appliqué sweatshirts. Don't mess.

"Good morning, Ms. McMinn. How are you?" I smiled warmly, hoping for a thaw on this nice autumn morning.

"As well as can be expected on a Monday, particularly considering the remarkable disrespect I have heard only this morning from America's youth. I assume you are here to speak with Dr. Willard?"

"Yes. I'll just wait until he's ready." I started toward a seat next to a sullen-looking boy in black. I couldn't help noticing we matched, though I think he was going for a slightly different effect.

Ms. McMinn cleared her throat and spoke into her phone. "Heidi Elliott here for you, Dr. Willard." She hung up and looked at her captors. "He'll be right with you, Mrs. Elliott. Micah, you're just going to have to wait. And it wouldn't kill you to sit up straight." I was fairly certain the Iron Maiden had actually starched her collar. I was also fairly certain I didn't own starch.

Micah grunted.

I sat down and noted with pleasure the familiarity of my surroundings. I looked around me at the office I'd whisked in and out of hundreds of times a day, checking my mailbox, submitting intercom announcements, asking McMinn for extra chalk, which she kept under lock and key with the Wite-Out and rubber cement. Even the presence of Micah in Black was oddly comforting.

The neglected sections of my brain kicked into gear, the ones independent of "-ie" words like blankie, nightie, and poopy. I couldn't wait to brush off the dust of my former self, the one in which I'd invested thousands of hours and dollars to educate. Not that I hadn't enjoyed my time with Nora. I wouldn't have done it any other way. But, just like pregnancy, there came a time when life had to return to normal.

"Aren't you the Spanish teacher who had a baby?" Micah was busy drawing some sort of gnome on his beat-up sneaker and didn't look up when he spoke.

"Yes, I am. My name is Mrs. Elliott."

"I registered for your Spanish II, second hour. But some dork is subbing for you. You should get a babysitter or something."

Nothing like the angst-shaded compliments of a sixteen-year-old.

"I'm up for next semester, actually," I said, watching the gnome acquire hair and a goatee. "Are you going to stick with it?"

Grunt. "Maybe."

Ms. McMinn's beady, carefully shadowed eyes peered over her computer. "Mrs. Elliott, Dr. Willard is ready for you. Micah, perhaps you could find better uses for ink."

I heard Dorothy muttering something about the Great Depression, which she was too young to have experienced but probably loved to reenact at home.

"Good to meet you, Micah," I said as I rose to go. "Give me a chance next semester."

"Adiós," he muttered to his sneaker.

I could work with that.

ℰ ᵹ ℰ

Dr. Willard opened his door as I approached. "Heidi! How's the new mommy?"

For a moment I panicked, thinking he was going to rub my belly.

During my pregnancy Dr. Willard had felt a strange and unwelcome freedom to touch my expanding midriff. I had split-second, heightened Jackie Chan awareness, readying myself to karate chop his pudgy little fingers. Fortunately Dr. W. was reaching for my hand, which is an acceptable custom in Western cultures and not nearly as intrusive as a belly rub.

"Hi, Dr. Willard. It's good to see you," I said, which was not entirely false. Dr. Willard was a very nice man, in his own school administrator sort of way. He had difficulty focusing on details like, say, curriculum, teaching philosophies, and critical thinking, but he was adept at other skills his job required. For example, he was very good at a select group of motivational speeches. I was certain Micah in Black was in for the "You can be *more*—just give it a try!" which included several "inspirational" stories involving Sam Walton, founder of Wal-Mart.

I wish I were making this up.

At any rate, I was not *un*happy to see Dr. Willard, which I felt was quite good enough. I sat in the chair he indicated. "How is your family?" I asked.

"Wonderful, wonderful," Dr. Willard nodded earnestly. "Bobby's doing very well at the U, studying communications and playing football, playing football. And Lisa's enjoying her last year of junior high. Keeping busy, keeping busy."

"And how is Mrs. Willard?" I asked. "I'm sure this is a busy time of year for her." Mary Jo Willard served as director of Springdale's annual Holly Daze Parade, a veritable orgy of tinsel, candy canes, and other forms of holiday merriment that made its way across town the third weekend in December. Mrs. Willard, fond of wearing hot pink and turquoise nylon running suits year-round, was very well suited to her job and to her husband. I'd found it best to avoid the woman like the plague, both for her morning-news-anchor personality and her uncanny ability to persuade people to volunteer for the ring toss or dunk tank.

"Oh, yes, yes. That Mary. Just can't keep her down. She's a live wire, that one!" Dr. Willard barked out a percussive laugh that didn't spread to his eyes. "So, Heidi, you're ready to come back to the halls of academia?"

"Yes, I am." My cell phone vibrated in my purse, and I had to bite my cheek to keep from answering it. Was it Lauren? Had she inadvertently given Nora peanuts before the recommended age of two and sent her unwittingly into a deep coma?

". . . and I'm sure you'll find everything in good order. Have you been in contact with her?" Dr. Willard was looking at me inquisitively.

Catch up, brain. What did he just ask?

"Um, in contact with . . . oh, Ms. Stillwell? My sub? Yes, of course. I mean, I plan on talking with her this morning when you and I are through."

Anaphylactic shock? Perhaps Nora's first bee sting and we didn't have one of those pens to counteract the allergic reaction?

I cast a furtive glance at my phone.

Dr. Willard paused; my phone stopped vibrating. "Heidi," he said, taking off his glasses and rubbing the red creases they'd left on the bridge of his nose. "Now, I want you to be sure you're ready for this, see. We've had many new mommies come back after their maternity leave thinking they're ready for the real world again, only to have them quit on us a few weeks into the semester." He raised bushy eyebrows, smirking. "Makes for quite the dilemma on the administrative side."

Feathers significantly ruffled, I forgot about my unanswered phone. I pulled myself up to my full height, which, while not imposing to many, easily equaled stocky Dr. Willard's, former shot put champion that he was.

"Dr. Willard, I assure you I'm ready to be back. More than ready. You don't need to worry about any divided attentions or lack of preparedness." Jerk, I added to myself. What decade did he live in that he had the moxie to insinuate women couldn't multitask? I did little to disguise the disdain on my face.

"Great," said Dr. Willard, disdain completely lost on him. He rose from his faux leather office chair. "I'll let you and Ms. Stillwell get caught up. Glad you're back, Heidi, glad you're back. I'll be happy to tell parents that our Minnesota Teacher of the Year 2004 is back to work at Springdale." He gave me a thumbs-up and flashed me his best I'm-still-your-boss grin as he showed me to his door. "Kiss that precious little bundle for me."

Sick.

"I sure will," I said, clutching my purse to my injured pride as I made my way past McMinn and Micah, who looked at me through his bangs.

"Boy or girl?" he asked.

"Sorry? Oh, girl. Nora. Her name is Nora." I pushed open the office door.

"Nice." Micah approved.

I smiled distractedly through the closing door and remembered the missed phone call that had caused me heart palpitations. Still muttering to myself about Willard's little pep talk, I retrieved the phone and looked at my caller ID. Jake.

"Jake," I said when he answered. "You called during my meeting."

I could hear him giving muffled instructions to an employee, and then, "Hi, Heids. I was just calling to see if you'd pick up my dry cleaning on your way home."

Dry cleaning? I made a mental note to add "maid" and "concierge" to my résumé. "Sure. And the meeting went fine, now that I know we have time to get an EpiPen for deadly allergic reactions and that 'mommies' are employment risks."

"That's great, hon. Thanks for the shirts." For all intents and purposes, he'd already hung up. "See you tonight."

"Right."

I dropped my phone back into my purse and headed for the foreign language hallway, breathing deeply and banishing thoughts of self-absorbed males, the glass ceiling, and Spanish-speaking gnomes.

I am so ready for this.

chapter/two

"Heidi! Are you back?" Rachel Davis accosted me with a smile as I passed the cafeteria. She wore a brown tailored skirt with a ribbed turtleneck sweater. She tucked glossy black hair behind her ears, revealing more of her round face. "It's so good to see you."

"Hi, Rachel. Thanks. It's good to see you, too." I smiled at a younger version of myself. I'd met Rachel the previous school year through a teacher mentoring program sponsored by the district. Fresh out of student teaching, Rachel had impressed me with her eagerness to learn and improve her teaching. "I'm back, but just for the morning. I'm here to firm up details of my return after the holidays."

"We've really missed you around here," Rachel said, shaking her head. She lowered her voice. "Janice Hoffman is filling in as school board liaison and is a *disaster*. And the curriculum task force decided just to adjourn until you came back."

My head swelled. "You're very kind to give me that much credit, Rachel."

"Oh, it's true," she gushed, earning herself a nice fruit basket for Christmas. "Springdale is so lucky to have you."

See, now? That's exactly what I was talking about. Elmo just couldn't give a girl that kind of affirmation. "Well, thank you," I said. "It'll be good to be back in the classroom."

Rachel nodded, smiling. "Then I'll see you in January." She turned to go. "Oh," she said as an afterthought. "How's your baby?"

"Nora's fine, thanks," I said. "She's growing like a weed."

Rachel shook her head. "I don't know how you did it, staying home all these months. I think I'd go crazy." She gave a wave and strode down the hall toward her classroom in the science wing.

I had my days, I thought, watching her go.

"*¡Siéntense, por favor! ¡Siéntense, chicos!*"

I entered the back door of my classroom to Ms. Stillwell's frantic commands. The woman could screech. Let's just say I wouldn't be asking her to record Nora's favorite lullabies any time soon. Think emu on meth.

She saw me enter and gave a quick nod with pursed lips. A Stillwell smile? "*Chicos*, it's time to begin. *Empezar. Empecemos. ¡Empiezo!*"

Third time is sometimes a charm, though not always when it comes to Spanish verb conjugation. La Señora tapped a foot clad in sensible shoes, pale hands clasped and resting on a plaid wool skirt. The room suited her more than it did me. Cinder block walls shone with industrial yellow paint. A cement floor was thinly swathed in navy blue rec room carpet. I'd always felt like a caged bird with the decor in my classroom, but Stillwell seemed a much better fit.

The Spanish II students filtered to their seats, unperturbed by Stillwell's fervent pleas. I had taught many of them in earlier semesters, and word slowly passed that I was sitting behind the last row of desks. Jessica Collins flashed me her bleached cheerleader smile accompanied by a perky wave. Micah in Black looked over his shoulder with a slow grin, and Ana López gave me a wry smile and rolled her eyes toward Ms. Stillwell.

"*Clase*, who can tell me why today is a special day?" Stillwell stood at attention behind some sort of lectern she must have dragged out of the janitor's closet. She looked over reading glasses at her charges.

Micah raised his hand.

"Yes, Pepe?" Ms. Stillwell asked, already bracing herself.

"Because it's the eighth consecutive Monday this year that Darren's come to school 'el hung-o over-o'?"

Darren Smits pummeled Micah in the arm, and Ms. Stillwell looked like she'd swallowed castor oil.

"Inappropriate response, Pepe," Ms. Stillwell sputtered. I thought she might need to sit down and breathe into a paper bag.

"*¿El Día de los Muertos?*" asked Lindsay Patterson, president of her class and ruthless on the volleyball court.

"*Sí*, Lupe. The Day of the Dead." Ms. Stillwell, though still breathing heavily, seemed to be recovering nicely. "This holiday, celebrated each year in Mexico, pays homage to the dead by honoring them with processions, prayers, and feasts." Stillwell was reading this word for word from something in front of her and therefore did not see Austin Michaels get pegged with a flying No. 2 pencil.

"One interesting element of this festival is the leaving of tokens and gifts by graves of the deceased," Stillwell continued, undeterred. "These are believed to be received by dead loved ones and used to ease their travels in the supernatural world."

"Creepy," Jessica said, not looking up from a poster she was making for Friday's pep rally.

"What's so creepy about it?" Ana asked. "We put flowers on graves all the time."

"Yeah, but I don't think my grandma's actually going to swoop by and pick them up when she's taking a stroll outside the pearly gates," Darren said, slouching so deeply into the tiny desk I thought he might break the thing into toothpicks.

"*Gringos* are so unbelievably narrow-minded," Ana said, fuming. She whirled around in her desk to face Darren. "Have you ever even been out of Springdale?"

Darren tried sitting up for emphasis but couldn't quite cut it. "What are you talking about, López? '*Gringos*'? You've lived in this country your whole ridiculous life! You're more *gringo* than I am."

I saw Micah chuckling to himself, not looking up from the unicorn tattoo he was inking onto his arm.

Ms. Stillwell had wisely sat down by now. "Now, *clase*," she said feebly, "let's remember to be courteous, even in our disagreements. Perhaps we should continue this discussion after we've all had a chance to read more about *El Día de los Muertos*."

She rose to pass out a thick packet of photocopied materials. "You may have the rest of the hour for tomorrow's assignment, which is to read the first twenty pages of this material." An overly dramatic teenage groan filled the room. "Don't worry. The reading is in English."

I mourned from my seat in the back of the room. It was a feat to get high school students riled up about anything unrelated to driving, dating, or illegal weekend ventures. A perfectly beautiful teaching moment, squelched and squandered right before my eyes.

I spent the last minutes of class jotting a note to myself on how exactly to repair the damage caused during my absence. And all I'd done was take a break to birth a child.

Qué desastre.

℮ ℈ ℮

"Did she cry?" my best friend, Annie, asked that afternoon. I'd called during her lunch break.

"Of course not," I answered, wedging the cell phone between my shoulder and my ear. I hefted Nora into an empty cart, fumbling for the germ-infested strap to buckle her up. We made our way toward the produce section of Tom's Ideal Grocery. Even above the piped-in instrumental of "Roxanne," I could hear Annie's chewing. "Whatcha eating there, Annie? Grape Nuts? Rock candy? Some scrap metal?"

"You are not very funny," Annie said as she continued her raucous munching.

I'd known Annie since we were wee things growing up in middle America. Together we survived the acne and braces of junior high, the catty females of high school, and the inexplicable males of college. I'd muddled through thick and thin with this girl, usually with me on the thicker end and Annie on the thin, at least in terms of kilograms.

"To answer your question, I am eating Power Mix II, an excellent source of protein, antioxidants, and Omega-3s. I've decided to run the Harvest Acres marathon next month."

In addition to maintaining a busy dental practice, Annie was a competitive long-distance runner. If I hadn't loved her so much, I definitely would have hated her guts.

"I don't think it's unreasonable to ask if Sergeant Stillwell cried," Annie said through her smacking. "I hear things in my line of work."

I pried an empty plastic produce bag from Nora's vise grip. No Heimlich maneuvers in Tom's today, thank you very much. "What, do people mistake you for Dr. Phil instead of Dr. Drill-Fill-and-Bill?" I snorted at my own joke.

"Hilarious. Very original. You should really consider taking your 'mock the dentist' act on the road." I heard more violent munching. "Just remember, people pay me a lot of money to wade through their saliva."

"Gross," I said, referring both to Annie's spit tolerance and the gum my daughter was trying to dislodge from our shopping cart. I distracted Nora with a teether and said to Annie, "All right, give it up. What'd you hear from your gossipy patients?" I'd tried, though not very hard, to take the high road, but I am not a girl who resists dishing with her best friend.

Nora tried to catch the eye of another cart rider, her face plastered with a slaphappy grin. The little boy stared at her unblinking, without one change of expression. Communication-deficient male, Stage One.

Annie's voice interrupted my smug psychoanalysis. "One very reliable source did mention that his *Español Dos* daughter complains nightly of the Señora's struggles." She paused to gulp down some Gatorade. I heard her swish it around in her mouth. Good grief.

I came to a stop by the root vegetables as Annie continued. "Two themes seem to dominate. Number One: Good teachers must be able to control a classroom, even during seventh period with all those wily sophomore football players on protein shakes. And Number Two: Good Spanish teachers must be able to speak Spanish."

I groaned. "Ouch. I feel horrible for her," I said, exchanging a graham cracker for the onion Nora was trying to eat through the bag. "She got roped into this whole thing by Dr. Willard, who was certain her three years of high school Spanish twenty-five years ago would suffice." Poor Stillwell. No one deserved the torture of teaching adolescents who knew you were clueless.

In the faint, cellular distance, I heard a hygienist page Annie for a patient check.

"I'll call you later, Heids," Annie said, her voice abruptly lowered, no trace of Power Mix II. "There may or may not be a beautiful man in Exam I who may or may not be looking for love in all the right places."

"Just try to work it out so that Nora's old enough to be a flower girl," I said. "And give the guy a break if he tries to chit-chat while you have your latexed hand in his mouth."

The buzz of Annie's electric toothbrush muddled her smart reply.

"Go ahead and finish your preventative care," I said. "Talk with you later, Dr. Love."

I hung up with a smile, hoping she was right about Exam I and that if he could look beyond his root canal, he'd know how to treat a woman better than those in Annie's long line of losers. The problem seemed to be that none of her former flames held their own in terms of intelligence, confidence, or the ability to do their own laundry.

By this time, Nora and I had progressed to canned goods, and I was loading up with applesauce, Nora's newest discovery in the breathtaking world of solid foods. I had stooped down to put a box of Raisin Bran on the bottom level when it happened.

I stopped midcrouch, horrified. I waited a moment, hoping against hope, but the wailing did not stop. On cue, the faucets turned on, full force.

I clutched a hand over my chest and looked up at Nora. Not a tear. I searched the aisle to find the author of my demise. The Wailer, a three-or-so-month-old a few paces away in bakery, cried above the soothing voice of his mother, who plucked him out of the infant car seat. The baby thrashed his little arms and legs, clamoring for attention, food, maybe sleep. Did it really matter what he wanted, for Pete's sake? Such details were irrelevant at this point because *my* breasts were more than willing to oblige this *stranger's* infant with milk, which was starting to shoot in copious amounts into my bra.

Heaping curses on the miracle of motherhood, I stood up, scurried to the driver's position, and started my sprint to the checkout. Nora giggled at the Dale Earnhardt speed, holding on for dear life as we flew through the bread aisle and past frozen foods. The wailing receded after a few moments, and I made a casual attempt at folding one arm across two saucer-size wet marks as I put my items on the conveyor belt. I became vaguely aware that Nora was slumped like Quasimodo in her seat, trying to eat the plastic red covering on the cart handgrip. Now was not the time to concern myself with trans-

mittable diseases, however, and I concentrated only on finding
my credit card with my remaining arm.

Stop the flow, I chided myself. Think nonmaternal
thoughts.

Barbara Walters.

Bill Gates.

Bill Gates naked.

Mission accomplished.

The faucets down to a drip, I lifted Nora out of her prone
position and took my receipt from the checkout girl, who
looked to be not a day over ten years old.

"Thank you and have a nice day," she said whilst popping
fluorescent green gum.

Nora and I headed to the exit, clutching each other for
different reasons entirely, but both extremely glad to be on
our way home.

℮ ℈ ℮

At one time in my life I'd savored the dinner hour. To wind
down after a long day at work, I'd change clothes, read the mail,
listen to Ella Fitzgerald or Nat King Cole. I'd nurse a glass of
Pinot Grigio while preparing, say, a stuffed pork tenderloin with
blue cheese mashed potatoes, steamed asparagus, a robust sourdough. Jake and I would sit down together, amble through a
quiet conversation, and often finish the meal with a home-baked
dessert involving shameless amounts of imported chocolate.

Enter Nora.

Tonight's entrée included something out of a box on which
was written, in DayGlo pink lettering, "Ready in Minutes!" I

gulped as I shoved the concoction into our ancient oven and prayed my mother-in-law would never know the depths to which I'd descended.

The sheer antiquity of our kitchen didn't help matters. In our remodeling efforts, Jake and I had gotten to both bathrooms and the master bedroom, but the kitchen still suffered from neglect. I'd been eager to overhaul the aesthetics—gold glitter countertops, stained brown sink, cheap cabinets, girly wallpaper—before Nora came along. But when we threw an infant into the mix, my motivation had plummeted.

I glanced at my daughter. She was vibrating like a jackhammer in her bouncy seat, God bless it. I reserved the *high* setting for this most fitful hour; the hysterical motion of it all seemed to shock her into momentary silence. Nora watched me with a glazed expression, and I joked aloud that maybe she'd like a beer to go with her La-Z-Boy.

"Nope, I'm cutting back," Jake said as he shut the front door behind him.

Nora snapped to attention and watched with a goofy grin as Jake walked to the kitchen and gave me a kiss.

"How was your day, hon?" I asked.

"Fine, thanks. How are my girls?" Jake scooped up Nora and tickled her neck with his nose. "Hey, ladybug. Did you miss me today?" Nora gurgled in response and swiped at Jake's glasses. "Wow, you *reek*! She's dirty, Heidi."

"Um, okay. Would you mind changing her?" You did, in fact, donate half of her genetic pool that fateful night, I thought. Jake's sense of equality became gravely dysfunctional when it came to diaper changing.

Holding Nora by her armpits well out in front of his body, Jake started toward the nursery. As he walked, he said over his shoulder, "How was your meeting at school?"

Biting back an expletive, I ran my fingers under cold water after burning them on the oven-hot pan. Could I not even handle a one-dish wonder these days?

"The meeting went fine. Everything's all ready to rock," I shouted, perhaps a little too aggressively. "In fact, I am so adept at multitasking I'm going to discuss my day with you while I bandage my wound, get your dinner on the table, feed our child, and write a letter to the freakin' president!"

I whirled around from the sink to see Jake and Nora, wide-eyed and wondering where this shouting woman had hidden their spouse/mother. I shut my eyes and tried desperately to think of an isolated beach, white sand, steel drums. . . .

"Wishoogee?" Nora asked.

"You said it, kid," Jake said. Then he looked at me warily. "Everything okay?"

"Fine. Just a little tired." I sighed, stepping around them. "Let's sit down and eat, okay?" I set our food and a gallon of milk on the table, grabbed some flatware and glasses, and sat down with a thud.

Jake put Nora in her chair, sat down, and took our hands. "Nora, what do you want to thank Jesus for tonight?"

I felt my stony, frantic heart begin to melt in one tiny corner.

"Oowoof," Nora said seriously.

"Okay," said Jake. "Let's pray. Thank You, God, for the gift of this day. We thank You for this food Mommy prepared for us, and we thank You for doggies. We love You, Jesus. Amen."

"Eeeen!" Nora trumpeted.

"Sorry about the outburst," I said, avoiding eye contact with my husband. I put Cheerios in Nora's bowl and cut up a banana onto her tray. "I'm still not quite used to the chaos of dinner time with child."

Jake shoveled up his first bite. My husband was lanky and scrappy, a former cross-country runner. He could also eat his body weight in one sitting. "Chaos?" he said around his food. "Everything seems fine when I get home. And then I'm here to help with Nora."

I swallowed hard. "First, honey," I said deliberately, "baby-sitters *help*. You *parent* because you are Nora's father. Secondly, everything *is* fine when you get home because I run around like a madwoman getting it that way so I can greet you with a clean house and a dewey fresh smile."

"Let's just have a nice meal, okay?" Jake asked wearily. "We can talk about this after Nora's in bed."

How did we get this way? I wondered as I helped Nora with her Cheerios. I didn't remember being in a foul mood before Jake got home. Jake's mere presence at the end of a day irritated me lately. Was it just the shifting dynamics of a family of three? How long could I coast on the excuse of postpartum hormones?

"So how was your day?" I asked, forcing my head to quiet long enough for a civil adult conversation.

Jake looked up from his plate. "Pretty busy. Things have been a little nutty ever since we landed the Van Fleet account."

Jake owned Elliott Paints and also contracted out painting jobs in the area. His newest project was with Jonathan Van

Fleet, a wealthy banker who dabbled in real estate and was building some condos on the north side of town.

"What's he like? Van Fleet, I mean," I asked as I took my first bite. Five point six minutes into the meal, in case anyone was keeping score.

"Interesting," said Jake. "Rather quiet, but very opinionated. Very well dressed. The word *dapper* would definitely apply."

"I hear his daughter is a knockout," I said, watching Nora squish her last banana morsel between doughy fingers.

"Yeah, she's pretty." Jake looked at his plate.

I waited, and then, "So you've met her?"

Jake buttered a piece of bread with great care. "Yeah, she comes with Jonathan to most of our meetings."

Nora interrupted our conversation with a whimper that grew quickly to a top-notch wail. Translation: Bath and bed, please. You two can box it out over the foxy banker's daughter later.

I rose from my chair and helped Nora out of hers. Heading to the bathroom, I said to Jake, "You go ahead and finish your meal. I'll put her to bed."

I couldn't exactly hear his response over Nora's feverish pitch, but I assumed he agreed with my plan. Balancing Nora on my hip, I fiddled with the bath temperature, then began to strip Nora of her play clothes and diaper. She cried miserably, the effects of a day too long for six-month-old coping skills.

"Okay, you're okay," I murmured to Nora, rocking her as we waited for her infant bathtub to fill. "We're okay," I added, hoping to convince us both.

chapter/three

If I had my way, every morning would dawn in early November. The air felt so clean, like it had been scrubbed by my Dutch grandma and hung to dry in the crisp orange and yellow sunshine of autumn.

At eleven o'clock—post morning nap, post violent diaper change, pre lunch—I held my daughter on our porch swing as we sang through Nora's Greatest Hits. We'd made it through the reggae, folk, and rap versions of "Itsy Bitsy Spider" and had moved on to a jazzy "Twinkle, Twinkle, Little Star." Nora gurgled along, sounding a bit like Liza Minelli in an aquarium.

We lived in a century-old house in a part of town that had experienced a sort of urban renewal. Our neighborhood was a residential gumbo, home to elderly people who'd lived there for decades, young families who brought fresh enthusiasm to tired, old houses, and a few nice gay men who were game to tolerate both tricycles and canes.

Jake and I had fallen head over heels for our two-story home and its warm oak floors, wide wood trim, and antique light fixtures. The house's age called for some allowances. For example, we couldn't exactly see each other after dark in the primitive lighting. We'd narrowly escaped divorce after removing wild floral wallpaper in four of the rooms. And walls collapsed if we tried to hang a picture. But we were young and full of naïve energy, and we chose character over ease.

Nora and I rocked back and forth, watching as the breeze lifted translucent yellow leaves off their perches and carried them gingerly to the ground. I was calculating in my head just how many bags we'd have to rake by the end of fall when a voice snapped me out of my wondering.

"Heidi?"

A tall man in jeans and a long-sleeved cotton shirt stood on our front walk. I squinted into sunlight to focus on his face, feeling my heart rate quicken dangerously beneath my ratty T-shirt as I realized who he was.

"Yes," I said slowly. "Ben?"

The man's eyes warmed and a comfortable grin spread across his face. "It's been a while, huh?" Ben made his way up the porch.

"Ben Cooper. Wow, it's great to see you," I said, standing while balancing Nora on my hip. I looked at her and said, "This is my little girl, Nora."

Ben leaned down and let Nora's fingers curl around his own. I stole the moment to check out what the years had done to him. Hair thick and dark, starting to have a sprinkling of gray, a curious improvement. As they had for all the years I'd known him, Ben's dark eyes crinkled with mischief, complimenting a wide smile orthodontists would covet.

"It's my pleasure to meet you, Miss Nora," Ben said. He studied her for a moment and said, "You have your mama's smile." He looked back at me.

My cheeks warming, I gestured to one of the Adirondacks. "Please, sit down. Can I get you something to drink?"

"Oh, no, I'll stay just a minute," he said as he lowered his body into the chair. "I'm beat, but I wanted to stop by before I passed out on the couch. If I can find the couch, that is."

Nora started to fuss in my arms, which were held at an awkward angle to avoid the Underarm Flab Effect. "Your couch is AWOL?" I set Nora down on the porch floor and handed her a plastic board book to gnaw. She'd started to sit without the protection of a pillow fortress, but I sat behind her as a buffer just in case.

Ben cleared his throat and massaged the day's beard. "Actually," he said, watching our trees rain down their leaves, "I moved today. I'm back in Springdale, and I've bought a house not far from here."

"You're kidding. Where is your new house?" I realized there was no car in our driveway.

"Well," he said, looking now at Nora, who was enjoying her Dr. Seuss appetizer, "I'm on Hollowbrook."

Not even five blocks away.

I cleared my throat. "I had no idea you were coming back."

My head was starting a slow spin. Do I welcome him to the neighborhood? He's an ex-boyfriend, three blocks away. No biggie, I insisted to myself. That was all a long time ago. I was a child, for Pete's sake. And now I *have* a child.

And a husband, I added hastily.

Ben fumbled with the citronella candle sitting on the arm of his chair. "My work has brought me to stranger places. I'm kind of excited to get the lay of familiar land again. My agent begrudgingly agreed it's a good move, albeit a tad unconventional."

Ben worked as a freelance photographer and was well regarded in his field. His work regularly appeared in major magazines and newspapers. Springdale thought of Ben as one of its golden boys. Last year Dr. Willard had Ben's AP photo put on a plaque in the high school student center, alongside other "famous" graduates, including a photo of 1981 Ice Fishing Champ Hal Lindstrom, holding with two hands his winning nineteen-pound pike.

"Well, I hope you're happy here. We're a far cry from Manhattan," I reminded him.

Ben's eyes shone as he laughed. "I know. I haven't had a good cup of coffee in days."

"You'll have to stop by for a cup sometime. I've been known to make a killer latte."

"I remember that." He looked at me for a moment and then stood. "I should run. My house is one big unpacked box." Ben started down the stairs and onto the front walk.

I stood up. "It's really good to see you, Ben. Welcome home." I couldn't help but smile, and he smiled back.

"Tell Jake I said hello," he said and then walked around the corner and was gone.

Nora was happily squishing ants between her pudgy fingers. I picked her up and said, "Let's go inside, peanut. Lauren will be here soon." I looked once more toward the street before I let the screen door slam behind me.

℮ ℈ ℮

"That sounds good," I said, closing my notebook. Ms. Stillwell was finishing up her review of the last eight weeks and giving me the lowdown of what was to come before my return after winter break. One thing about Stillwell: That woman could move through material like MacArthur through the Philippines. Whether or not the students had retained anything remained to be seen, but the pace at which they were clipping through those vocab lists and verb tenses was mind-numbing.

Ms. Stillwell folded her glasses and placed them in her needlepoint case. "I hope you will find your classes adequately prepared for your return," she said, studying her hands.

"I'm sure I will," I replied. "Thank you, Ms. Stillwell, for being so willing to teach this semester. I greatly appreciate the extra time it has given me with my daughter."

Ms. Stillwell nodded, still looking down. I waited, sensing we might not be as ready to rock as I'd thought.

"I'll actually miss them," she said at last. "I'll miss the little hellions." Ms. Stillwell bit her lip while her eyes filled.

"Well, I'm sure they'll miss you, too, Ms. Stillwell. You've spent a lot of time with them, learning together—"

"I'm a *failure!*" Stillwell yelped, coming awfully close to the emu. "They *abhor* me, *despise* me!"

Oh, Good Lord, I prayed, please don't let her nose run.

I gathered my thoughts before offering, "Ms. Stillwell, teenagers are the masters of disguise. Very rarely do they show authentic, unguarded affection, even when they feel it." Grasping for straws, I knew, but not entirely untrue.

"You probably can't identify," she said as she sniffed into a real-life handkerchief, embroidered with peonies and irises. "You're young, fresh. They think you're *funny*. Believe me, they've mentioned it more than a few times."

Big, liquidy sniff.

"I just can't bear the thought of going back to my cross-stitching club, for pity's sake. Not that I don't appreciate a fine piece of handiwork, but these kids have some *kick* to them." She sighed with resignation. "And there are other things." She lowered her eyes, letting her voice trail off.

I waited, but she said no more. I considered keeping my mouth shut, letting the confessional moment pass without further embarrassment, but then thought, What the hay. She's *snorting* in front of me. It's not like we can worry about dignity in moments like this.

"Ms. Stillwell," I began, "I am so pleased to hear you've loved teaching my students. They are amazing people and I've missed them, even the glue snorters, the gum poppers, and the smart alecks. I wonder, though — do you think *they* know you've enjoyed them?"

She cleared her throat. "Perhaps not." Her lip was twitching like a disoriented Elvis. "Perhaps I've been a bit stern with the pip-squeaks."

Perhaps?

"Try communicating a little more joy and a little less fear," I suggested gingerly. She *was* Señora Stillwell, after all; she could probably beat me up. "You still have lots of time together. You are the teacher and you are the adult, but you can learn from your students as well."

Stillwell folded her wet hanky and put it back into her pocketbook, which reminded me why I don't use hankies. "I'm sorry to burden you with this, Mrs. Elliott. I really didn't know I had it in me to show such emotion. Frankly," she said, shuddering, "it's rather disconcerting."

Tell me about it, sister. "I'm grateful for your honesty."

I thought about covering her hand with mine in a gesture of solidarity, but Rome wasn't built in a day, people.

She stood abruptly. "I need to stop by the powder room before the beginning of sixth period." She pushed back her chair, patted her tight gray curls, and picked up her papers.

"Thank you again for meeting with me," I said as I stood. "Please don't hesitate to call if you have any questions or concerns before I return in January."

"Yes, of course," she said, already scuttling for the door. "Enjoy the rest of your time off."

"Ms. Stillwell," I called after her.

She looked at me.

"Never underestimate the power of humor."

Stillwell stood with her hand on the doorknob, her expression quizzical. Then she nodded quickly, pursed a Stillwell smile, and left.

Watch out, pip-squeaks, I thought. Nothing like a cross-stitcher on a mission.

☙ ☙ ☙

When I walked through our front door a half hour later I was pleasantly surprised to be greeted by Jake. His light blue eyes lit up when he saw me, and he enveloped me in a warm hug.

"Welcome home," he said, leaning down to kiss me.

"You're home early," I said, holding on to him a moment longer. "What's the occasion?" I shed my jacket while he returned to the kitchen, where he was busy putting little packages into our worn picnic basket. Nora sat watching him from her position on the kitchen floor. She wielded a wooden spoon, which she banged on the linoleum whenever she remembered she was armed.

"The occasion is one of our last picnic-friendly afternoons of the season and my desire to spend it with my wife and baby girl instead of in a chemically induced haze at a paint store." Jake wore jeans, a fleece pullover, and running shoes, which I hoped he'd use to chase me. I sucked in my stomach, remembering my figure's recent southerly migration.

"Hello, peanut," I said softly, getting down on the floor to kiss Nora's forehead. "Did you have a nice time with Lauren while Mommy met with Ms. Stillwell?"

"Sosososos," replied Nora with an earnest expression.

"So-so, eh?" Jake said. "Your mom and dad can do better than so-so. Five minutes, Heids?"

"Great," I said, disrobing as I walked to our bedroom. The tourniquet syndrome was slowly diminishing, but donning my pre-Nora clothes still put me in mind of two pigs fighting under a blanket. Much more comfortable in a green hoodie and blue jeans, I reemerged to find Jake stuffing the picnic basket into the bottom compartment of Nora's stroller. Nora chewed gamely on the safety strap, happy to be on her way outside.

"I don't know what we'll do this winter," I said, holding the front door for Jake as he pushed Nora ahead of him. "This girl is a park ranger in the making, she loves the outdoors so much."

"There are always snowsuits and mittens," Jake replied, lifting his face to the autumn sunshine.

"You lead," I said, content with this unexpected family time. Jake led us on a lazy stroll toward our neighborhood park.

We weren't the only ones seeking one last fling before the winter cold. A group of university students ran circles around each other in an Ultimate Frisbee game, while several older couples chatted on wooden benches. The playground was packed with young families. Nora stared with round eyes at several two-foot furies running around the swings and slides.

"Should we take her over to the baby swing?" I asked, unbuckling Nora's strap. She kicked her legs in excitement as she watched the bright colors of the Frisbee, the playground, and fall's last flowers swirl around her.

"I'm right behind you," Jake said as he maneuvered our SUV-imitation stroller toward the path leading to the playground. Nora and I took the direct route and ascended the grassy hill.

Nora was squealing during her third ascent in the swing before I realized Jake was nowhere to be found. I shaded my eyes from the sun, scanning the crowded play area for a glimpse of a stroller-accompanied man in polar fleece. There were roughly fifty-four of them. Then my eyes stopped abruptly on two men talking, both in fleece, but only one was my husband.

The other was Ben Cooper.

Oh, dear.

Quickly I looked back at Nora, hoping when I checked again the whole scene would have been a nasty mirage, some sort of hallucination brought on by excessive sunlight and fresh air. I cooed with my daughter for a while, and when I looked up, I locked eyes with Jake, who gave a courteous wave. In general, I found it to be a bad sign when your husband's actions could be described as courteous. Ben smiled at me, said some words to Jake, and the two of them headed toward our turf by the swings.

"Heidi, look who I bumped into." Was that a smirk on Jake's face?

I smiled indulgently at my husband and then turned to Ben. "How are you, Ben?" Did I mention the unusually warm temperature in the park that day?

"Fine, thanks," Ben replied, looking at Nora. "Hi, cutie." She slobbered a friendly hello.

"How's the unpacking coming along?" I asked Ben, simultaneously wishing I'd actually looked in a mirror before leaving our house. For Jake's sake, of course.

"Ridiculous, the amount of stuff I've accumulated in my short life," Ben said with a wry smile. "But I'm settling in, bit by bit."

I realized Jake was staring at me. "Heidi," he said, "Ben tells me he stopped by our house the other day."

I must have been neglecting my swinging responsibilities because Jake moved into the pusher position. Nora, though thrilled for the extra action, was reaching precipitous heights under her father's hand.

I cleared my throat and went for nonchalance. "Didn't I tell you about that, hon?"

Jake looked only at Nora while he shook his head.

I continued, "Ben stopped to let us know he was in the neighborhood for good. I'm afraid I wasn't very hospitable, though, since I made him stay on the porch, outside, in open view of the neighborhood."

Ben started to look vaguely uncomfortable, and I wondered when I'd stop talking.

Nora catapulted through the air as Jake increased the force of his push. I started to become concerned about infant whiplash.

"Well, Ben," Jake said, with an empty smile, "I hope you like being back in Springdale. I know there will be a lot of people glad to have you back." Jake, I was sure, would put himself at the top of a different list.

Ben rubbed his five o'clock shadow. I was starting to suspect he used one of those razors that ensured a leftover scruffy look. "Thanks, Jake," he said, slapping the newspaper he was carrying against his open palm. "I'd better get to my reading. This is my last day of grace before jumping back into work mode." He nodded at Jake and tried to ruffle Nora's hair as she whizzed upward. "See you, Heidi," he said to me and walked away from us, dodging a hurtling two-year-old on his way off the play mat.

Jake continued to push Nora at a rate imperceptibly slower than the speed of light. After a few moments, I said, "Would you like me to take over?" So we can prevent permanent spinal cord damage?

Without a word, Jake walked to a nearby picnic table and started setting out our dinner. He'd brought all our summer favorites: strawberries, a few cheeses, grapes, Greek olives, smoked salmon, and a loaf of challah. Dessert would be a Wizard Whip at the nearby Dairy Freeze, if we were still on speaking terms by that time.

I lifted Nora out of the swing to wild protests, calmed only by stuffing a pear slice into her pudgy hand. I popped a couple grapes into my mouth and said, "Jake, I'm sorry I didn't mention Ben's visit."

Jake just chewed his salmon sandwich.

I tried again. "Honey, you know he means nothing to me. He is ancient history."

"You should have said something, Heidi." Jake looked me in the eye. I winced. "I just can't believe it never crossed your mind."

Now I took a turn with my sandwich.

"This isn't just any ex-boyfriend. You *lived* with him, Heidi," Jake stopped, visibly bothered by taking a trip down this memory lane. "You two have a long and involved past, and I feel extremely uncomfortable knowing a man who's seen my wife naked is back in town. *And* my new neighbor. *And* visiting my wife and daughter when I'm not home." Jake stopped himself. He rubbed his eyes, all of a sudden looking and sounding exhausted. "I can't believe I'm having to ask you to be honest with me after all these years."

"Jake, I really don't think this is such a big deal. Besides," I mumbled, picking at a strawberry, "I said I was sorry." Nora took the strawberry away from me and set about staining another shirt.

"I don't want 'sorry,'" he said wearily. "I want honesty." He looked at me for a moment. "If honesty doesn't strike you as 'such a big deal,' we're in for some hard knocks." He looked as if he had more to say but fell silent as he began picking up our picnic and putting it back in the basket. "It looks like rain," he said by way of explanation. "We can finish dinner at home."

Nora, by now bathed in red, did not smile at her dad as he put her back in the stroller. Jake kept his face straight as well, and he began to push her out of the park.

I rose from the picnic table and fell in behind them. Lifting my eyes, I scanned the sky.

Suspicions confirmed. Not a cloud in sight.

chapter/four

Things change with the birth of a child. Life insurance suddenly makes sense, for instance. Prime-time television becomes offensive. The words "sleeping in" elicit nothing but nostalgia.

It shocked me to find the force of impact was not gender neutral. Fathers were allowed casual forays into the world of parenting, coming and leaving as they pleased. They relegated themselves to car seat installation, Little League sign-ups, and the establishment of far-off college funds. The brave ones complained about dried-up sex lives. And then they made their convenient exit, back to normal lives as accountants, vacuum salesmen, podiatrists.

New mothers, though, might as well have grown two spinning heads and moved to the Bermuda Triangle. Perhaps building on nine months of uterine sharing, mothers were the new axis on which the universe hinged. We fed, we cleaned, we wiped, we soothed, or, in a pinch, we had better leave instructions and a map.

Perhaps my most jarring initiation to the world of motherhood was the realization that my body still looked like an extraterrestrial's even after Nora had vacated the premises. While I *could* shoot milk the length of a football field, my Kegels were not, shall we say, what they used to be. Stretch marks created a spaghetti squash roadmap across my entire body. And if I ever made the mistake of looking in a mirror while naked, I heard myself gasp.

Incidentally, I didn't remember being warned of any of these side effects during sex ed class in junior high. Think of the sudden rise in teenage abstinence if a group of postpartum women stormed seventh grade classrooms and lifted up their shirts.

What's a girl to do, really? Go down with the ship? Chalk up another one to Mother Nature? Hibernate?

I did what any best friend of a skinny triathlete dentist would do. I called Annie.

"Excellent," she said. "I'll meet you at the gym at noon."

When I arrived at Wayne's Fitness World, Annie met me at the front desk. Hair swept back in a neat ponytail, clothed in black yoga pants and a pink fitted tank, lean arms exposed, Annie should have been on Wayne's promotional brochures. I noticed several males checking her out appreciatively as they strutted by.

Oblivious, Annie took Nora's carrier car seat from me and handed me a towel. "You can use my locker," she said, nodding at the coat I'd pulled around my oversize T-shirt and baggy sweats. "I'll take Nora to child care."

I followed Annie. "Are you sure there are good people in there? I mean, I'm sure they mean well, but pink eye is *rampant* this season, and there's strep, RSV, mad cow . . ."

Annie turned around. "Heidi," she said with the calm of a kindergarten teacher. "I know every single one of the caregivers here. They are well qualified and religiously committed to anti-bacterial hand gel. Now, go get dressed and meet me by the free weights."

I leaned down to kiss Nora, who pulled out roughly one-eighth of the hair on my head. "I love you. I'll miss you."

Annie rolled her eyes. "Okay, enough *Steel Magnolias*. Come on, Nora. Mommy needs some Heidi time." I watched as her expertly toned rear sashayed away with my child.

A few minutes later, I stood waiting for Annie, not at all comfortable with the mirror-flanked walls. Seriously, did anyone *really* need so many reminders of how they looked when sweaty? I caught a reflection of Annie striding toward me and the wake of double takes she produced.

"Okay, ready?" She picked up a nearby clipboard and scribbled something in her dentist scrawl. She bounded past me and said over her shoulder, "I thought we'd weigh in first, just to get a starting point."

I stopped dead in my tracks. "You thought *we'd* weigh in?" I whispered fiercely, panic rising in my voice. "Annie, those of you who have not experienced the joys and trials of pregnancy-induced weight gain may take lightly the public 'weigh-in.'" I'd started to hiss. "I, however, would rather be *flogged*."

"Wow," Annie muttered, shrugging shoulders made for strapless dresses. "Suit yourself. I just thought you'd like to chart your progress." She headed back to the weights, shedding the clipboard as she walked.

"I just want to try this whole thing out, okay?" I asked, following her to the bench press. "It's been a very long time, and I'd rather break it in slowly."

Annie was putting weights on the bar. Each one looked like it weighed as much as I did at thirty-two weeks of pregnancy. "Heidi," she said as she finished, looking at me. "I'm only trying to help. You need to feel like *you* again. Exercise will help you feel like a woman who is also a mom, instead of always feeling like a mom who happens to be female in her spare time."

Point taken, though not without resistance. I sighed. "Okay," I said. "You have me for an hour."

"Great," Annie said, trotting to pick up her clipboard. "Let's start with the bench. Lie down."

☙ ❧ ☙

"I actually think it helps when I moan," I said to Jake as I turned over in bed that night. I noticed a throb in a back muscle I hadn't known existed in mammals. Shifting again, my center of pain migrated to somewhere near my groin. In general, I didn't think anything should migrate near my groin unless it was Jake.

He chuckled. "Annie really worked you, huh? That's what you get for working out with a triathlete."

"Thank you for your show of sympathy," I said through gritted teeth. My teeth even hurt.

"It's good to be sore, hon," Jake said as he finished his bedtime sit-up regime. Why do I surround myself with these people? "Soreness shows you worked your muscles enough to make a difference."

"I certainly feel different," I said, starting to whine. "How am I going to lift Nora tomorrow? Unlike the one in this room who escapes to a paint store every morning, *my* parenting work is never done."

"Just take it easy," Jake replied, ignoring the subtle jab. "Try not to pick her up more than necessary."

I guffawed as much as was possible, given my condition. "That's very funny. And spoken by a man whose job doesn't involve a six-month-old whirling dervish." I made no attempt to make room for him as he joined me in bed.

"I know what you need," Jake said, snuggling up to me. "You need some love from your husband." He kissed my neck.

"Certainly you aren't serious," I said, playing dead.

Jake kept kissing, heading to my shoulders, which I hoped were significantly buffer than the last time he'd kissed them. "Mmmm," he murmured. "I love a woman who can stand a tough workout *and* raise my child, all in a day's work."

I rolled slightly toward him, knowing I was nailing my own coffin by that miniscule gesture. I smiled wryly. "Do you always get your way?" I asked, returning his kiss.

"Mostly," he said. "Or at least one time out of ten."

That seemed like a truthful ratio, particularly since Nora. I tried not to feel guilty about the drought and instead enjoy being touched, even with my extra pounds and acute need for Advil.

"Do you wish I looked like Annie?" I asked.

"Shut up," Jake said.

And for once, I did.

℮ ℈ ℮

The next morning, I rolled all my inflamed muscles out of bed and shuffled into Nora's room. Her voice on the baby monitor had awakened me, against my will since it was still dark and just after six. Amazingly, my daughter was rip-roarin' ready to go at this delicate hour. She sat up in her crib and greeted me with a gummy grin flanked by rosy cheeks.

"Morning, sweet girl," I said, lifting her out of her crib and enduring violent protests from my abs, shoulders, and arms. "How's my baby?" I snuggled into the folds of her neck.

Nora got right to business and yelped her desire for breakfast. I sat down in the nursery glider, alarming my quads, calves, and hamstrings. I could hear Jake starting the shower and tried with earnest to remember a time when I began my day with a hot shower, followed by a bagel, the paper, and a mug of caffeinated coffee that wouldn't backfire in my breast milk.

Nope. Couldn't place it.

I let my gaze drop to Nora, who had closed her eyes in deep contentment, focusing solely on the wonders of Mom, the short-order cook. Looking at her I was tempted to conclude that *I* was the one to envy, even without the bagel.

Ten minutes later, Jake surfaced in the kitchen, where Nora had begun her "big girl" breakfast of Crispix, no milk. Though little of the cereal completed the long and arduous journey to her mouth, she was determined nonetheless and screwed up her little face in concentration.

"Oh, what a beautiful morning," Jake crooned in his best Curly from *Oklahoma*. He danced over to me like the white man he was. "It really *is* a lovely morning, is it not?" he said into my ear, biting it playfully.

"Daddy," I scolded, looking at Nora, "don't be a dirty old man in front of innocent babes. Right, Nora?" Nora was trying the mass quantity approach, stuffing sixteen Crispix into her mouth at once, banking on best odds that one would eventually make it down the hatch.

Jake hummed as he scooped sugar onto his Grape Nuts. "What's on the docket for today, ladies?" he asked through a mouthful.

"Well," I said, cutting up a pear for Nora, "I thought we might take a trip to the mall, maybe pick out a birthday gift for Auntie Annie. She turns thirty next week. What about you?"

Jake gulped down a glass of orange juice. "We have a big meeting with Van Fleet. I guess he has some concerns about the palette, even though he gave us free reign with color. You never know with his type. He acted like he couldn't care less, but the bottom line is that he's accustomed to running people's lives. And what could a lowly painter know, I ask you?" Jake turned to Nora for some support. "What do you think, peanut? Who knows more: painter or banker?"

"What about banker's daughter?" I asked, making every effort to sound casual as I bit into my toast. "Does she get involved?"

"Jana's his only saving grace," Jake said as he put on his coat. "She's kind of his own personal diplomat. I don't know what we would have done to this point without her."

I swallowed my dry bite, took a long draw of juice. "It's good you appreciate her," I said, not without just a smidge of irony. "Women love to be appreciated."

"Well, I'm sure her father appreciates her, too," Oblivious Husband responded. "He has to know she keeps his PR dealings above water." Jake kissed Nora on the top of her head. "Bye, sweetheart. Be nice to your mom today."

He came toward me and kissed me in the same exact spot as Nora's smooch. "Love you," he said and walked toward the door.

I jumped up, much to the chagrin of my aching body. "Wait," I said, following him. "Kiss me like I'm your wife, not your daughter," and I laid one on him, morning toast breath and all.

Jake pulled away and smiled. "See," he said, "I *knew* you thought it was a beautiful morning."

He let the screen door slam behind him but not before I heard him whistling on his way to the car.

Good, I thought. Send him out happy so he remembers all day who's waiting for him at home.

chapter/five

Prior to Nora, I really didn't have much of a taste for shopping malls. For one thing, a high school teacher occupies a humble position on the monetary food chain. Mostly, though, I avoided shopping because of time. I worked a lot, Jake worked a lot, and when we weren't working, the last place I wanted to spend my time was the mecca for materialism, consumer greed, and full-color displays of emaciated models with synthetic breasts and swollen lips.

But in the months since Nora's birth, I'd become a mall rat. The thrill of seeing other humans, knowing what was in style, even if I couldn't fit into any of it, and the possibility that Nora would fall asleep in her stroller — all these things far outweighed any pious reservations.

After careful research, I'd concluded the best place to shop was Burke's department store. The abundance of polished marble and sparkling glass made me feel like Annie on her first visit to Daddy Warbucks. The salespeople were kind, always schmoozing with Nora and proclaiming her stunningly beautiful, even when she had biscuits caked in her eyelashes. And no Michael Bolton or Bangles Muzak in Burke's. Just a little old lady milking the ivories with Gershwin and Porter classics.

But rising to the top of this venerable list of perks was the Women's Lounge. Bigger than my first three apartments, the Lounge welcomed shoppers with velvet chairs and fresh floral arrangements. Here a shopper could avail herself of a changing table with diapers and warmed wipes provided. She could nurse her baby without fear of permanently scarring hapless security personnel. During those Women's Lounge moments, I asked God to continue to bless America and to forgive me for being shallow.

The promise of a Lounge visit lay before us as Nora and I ambled through Burke's that afternoon searching the shelves for Annie's gift. Thirty was a big birthday, a rite of passage out of the turbulent twenties and into total self-awareness and a slower metabolism. I marveled at all Annie had accomplished in her three decades, the woman she had become, the way she loved my family. A perfect gift was definitely the order of the day.

We stopped at the jewelry counter. Something classic? Contemporary? Annie wasn't exactly pearls and lace. Nora lounged in her stroller staring at the ceiling lights and likely burning her retinas, but giving me a chance to make an informed decision. I had asked the salesgirl to show me several turquoise pieces when I saw someone approach out of the corner of my eye.

"Heidi! What a joy to see you!" I turned to see Molly Langdon, dressed from head to toe in polka dots. Polka dot sweater, polka dot Capri pants, polka dot mules. Even a polka dot baseball cap trimmed in silver sequins. Molly had introduced herself to me a few weeks prior at the church Jake and I attended. I'd seen her plenty of times before, as she often gave congregational announcements, usually involving ladies' teas, luncheons, and other such horrors.

"Molly, how are you?" I said, breathing through my mouth to avoid vertigo.

Nora looked like she'd been hypnotized.

"I'm well, thanks be to God. He's so good!" she said, eyes twinkling. "And how's this little angel?" Molly stooped down to Nora's level. She patted Nora's cheek, though the action went unheeded by Comatose Baby, still suffering from the polka dots.

"She's doing well," I said, trying to distract Nora's gaze with a chewy toy I shoved in her face. It couldn't be good for infants to feel like they're on crack. "We're out to find a birthday gift for a friend, wandering a bit."

"Well, Heidi, I certainly won't keep you two," Molly said, her perfectly made-up face breaking into a wrinkle-free smile despite her fifty-some years. Her thick highlighted hair was pulled into a neat ponytail. Blue eyes shone behind glittered magenta frames. If we'd known each other better, I would have loved to ask her about Botox. Did it hurt? How about maintenance?

". . . Wednesday evenings at seven o'clock, and we'd *love* to see you there." I tuned back in to hear the end of Molly's invitation. "It's a group of moms, many of them stay-at-home, and we've found it's just *priceless* to have some support during these precious years. I know when my own children were young, I really could have used a social *outlet*." Molly's bright pink lipstick mimicked precisely the purse she carried. This woman accessorized.

"Thanks so much for thinking of me," I hedged. A group of women getting together to sing "Kumbaya" and talk about their feelings? Sounded like a blast, but count me out. "I'll see if I can make it one of these days." I busied myself rummaging around in Nora's diaper bag for an object unidentified even to me. Is it possible to lie with body language?

"*Won*derful!" Molly tilted her head to one side like a beauty queen. Maybe the dots were wearing me down. "I'll look forward to seeing you *soon*. Remember, all meetings are at my home. Bring nothing but yourself," she finished cheerily.

"It's nice seeing you, Molly."

"You girls have a great time shopping. See you Sunday!" She winked at me before bouncing away.

"Wow, lovey," I said to Nora. "Nice lady, but too many dots." My precious time with turquoise squandered, I pushed Nora toward the Women's Lounge, trying to avoid the imminent hunger hysterics. By the time I'd passed active wear, Molly and her invitation had already left my mind.

☙ ☙ ☙

That Sunday I sat in a pew alone waiting for Jake to join me after parking the car. Nora played with her "friends" in the nursery, other wee ones she would drool on, cry with, and stare at for the next hour and a half, and none of whom she would remember by next week. Very similar to college beer parties.

Jake slipped in beside me, laying his black leather Bible next to him on the pew. While I wasn't exactly sure of the location of my own Bible, which I'd received at my confirmation in 1988, Jake had begun keeping his copy on the bedside table, and I'd caught him opening it up several mornings. Frankly, I was stupefied by his interest in a book that was written by crusty, bearded men thousands of years ago and that included words like "verily," "saith," and "begotten." I saw church more as a tidy Sunday ritual, one that smelled good and looked good and that I hoped would teach Nora a few morals along the way.

"Hi," saith Jake, slipping his arm around me and resting it on the mahogany bench. He smiled and nodded to a few people he knew. For my part, I gave strict attention to my bulletin. I'd noticed Molly Langdon and her husband, Dan, enter and sit in the section across from us. Molly, swathed in chartreuse linen and a beaded scarf, had started her own scan of the room. As I wanted nothing more of the Moms' Group invites, I kept my eyes down.

Pastor Isles, the music man, strode to the podium and asked us to stand and sing the first hymn. The organ swelled and Jake joined in with his baritone, seeming to understand and even appreciate something called a "bulwark." I like to sing, so this part was the least painful for me, even with mighty fortresses and Martin Luthers.

I missed most of the sermon due to my note taking, not on the words of Pastor Smits, but on my meal planning for the week. Jake took notes too, but they seemed to be more directly related to the topic at hand, which the bulletin announced was "Grace Under Fire." Sounded dangerous.

Pastor Isles closed the service with the doxology and dismissed us to a triumphant little ditty on the pipe organ. Jake and I made our way to the back and had nearly cleared the double doors when Molly materialized in all her beaded glory.

"Heidi!" she gushed. "I'm so *glad* I ran into you. Jake, how *are* you?" She reached out her manicured hand to shake Jake's rough painter's mitt. Some of this week's work lingered on his knuckles, even after multiple scrubbings with mineral spirits.

"Hi, Mrs. Langdon," Jake said with a warm smile. "Where's your sidekick?"

"Danny?" Molly batted away the mere thought with her acrylics. "Oh, he's such a *baby*. Always heads straight to the doughnuts and coffee, usually halfway through the doxology." She laughed and rolled her eyes. "The man fought in Vietnam but good *luck* getting him to go a full four hours between meals."

I took Jake's arm and began steering us toward the lobby. "It's good to see you, Molly. We'd better relieve the nursery workers."

"Of course, dear," she said, walking with us. This woman was tenacious. "Just wanted to let you know we'll be starting a new topic this Wednesday at Moms' Group. We'd love to have you *any* time, but this week is a fresh slate for all of us, so I think you'd be especially at *ease*."

"What's Moms' Group?" Jake asked, looking at me.

Molly answered, "We get together each week at my home, Jake. Just a way for busy moms to take time to get some spiritual and social *nourishment*." She winked. "And the husbands always approve because we are ready to be nice again when we get home from a night with the girls."

Jake's eyes sparked, thinking it might increase his odds of getting lucky, no doubt. "Sounds great. She'll be there."

"Wonderful!" Molly exclaimed, clapping her perfect hands. "See you Wednesday, then, Heidi. Seven at my house — we're in the book!"

"I'll have to check my calendar, find child care," I stammered, digging my nonmanicured, stubby fingernails into Jake's arm.

He ignored my attempt to inflict pain and chirped, "I'll babysit. Don't worry, honey. You deserve a night out."

Dead painter walking.

"Good to see you both," said Molly, probably feeling victorious. She gave me a side hug before walking away to join Dan at the doughnuts.

I beelined to the nursery, dragging Jake with me. "Let's not talk with any more church people this morning, okay?" I hissed.

"What?" Jake asked, bemused. "You'll have a great time. You're always saying you miss being able to just take time for a cup of coffee or to visit a bookstore. Here's your chance."

"A cup of coffee?" I asked incredulously. "Jake, do you know what you just committed me to? The First Lutheran Whiners' League, that's what. Those women are going to drive me nuts." I huffed down the Sunday school hallway.

"Heidi, you don't even know them yet," Jake said, schlepping along behind me. "Besides, Mrs. Langdon is really nice and I'm sure will make you feel very welcome. She'll probably have food."

"Unbelievable," I muttered quietly. We joined the line of parents waiting to pick up their little ones. "I'm doomed to a night with the church ladies and you try to comfort me with the prospect of free food. Maybe *you* should go and I'll stay with Nora."

"Hi, sweetie," Jake said as the nursery worker handed Nora over the counter to him. "Did you learn about Jesus today?" He kissed her and she slobbered her thanks all over his cheek.

"Thank you," I said to the worker, a smiling man with white hair and a sunshine-shaped name tag pinned to his golf shirt. The tag read, "God Loves Kids and So Do We!" He had written "Jim" in marker below.

"You are welcome," Jim said, patting Nora tenderly on the head with a weathered hand. "Nora's a very good girl. She loves music, I think. And other kids' graham crackers." He chuckled and handed me Nora's diaper bag.

"Both those traits come directly from her mother," I said, smiling back at Jim. I liked any male retiree who was willing to spend Sunday morning with a roomful of dirty diapers in progress.

"See you next week, Nora," Jim said, and Jake helped Nora wave back.

"See?" Jake said as we walked away. "Not all church people are weirdos." Nora clung to his neck as we wove through the hallway and out to our car.

"If Jim goes to Moms' Group, I'll go," I retorted.

Jake laughed. "Are you kidding?" he asked. "Those piranhas would eat that sweet old man alive."

chapter/six

Even scarier than group therapy is group therapy with all women.

Wednesday night at 7:02 I turned onto Magnolia Circle and saw a line of minivans parked outside a mammoth limestone two-story. After maneuvering my car into an open spot on the street, I idled a moment before turning off the ignition. Deep breath, I thought. Pretend you're meeting a group of freshmen on the first day of school. Then again, what kind of a case am I that a room full of acne-riddled, hormone-ravaged freshmen is easier to face than an innocent gathering of church moms?

With a plaintive sigh, I grabbed my purse and got out of the car.

"Welcome, welcome!" Molly trilled as she opened her wide front door. The vaulted foyer was warmly lit, showcasing three abstract paintings that hung in a descending line with the staircase. A life-size fountain depicting a young girl holding calla lilies stood behind Molly, filling the atrium with the soft sounds of bubbling water.

"Mind the water feature," Molly said, stepping lightly around Fountain Girl. "She's beautiful but a *tripping hazard*."

The closest I'd come to a water feature in my life was having a heart-to-heart with Stillwell. That and maybe Nora's tendency to weep, salivate, and urinate without advanced warning.

Molly led me into a bright kitchen filled with women. I forced my feet to follow the hostess, knowing that without extra effort I'd bolt right back past the calla lilies and out the front door. A bevy of women stood chatting in twos and threes around an island blanketed in shiny black granite. The walls were a warm bagel color; a tiled floor held up the room in terra-cotta, green, and slate. Frankly, I was surprised to encounter such a subdued schema, given Molly's clothing preferences.

"Heidi, what can I get you to drink?" Molly asked, heading for a pretty granite cove with a sink, mini-fridge, and empty wine rack overhead. "Soda? Lemonade? Iced tea?"

How about a dry martini, two olives? I thought. "I'd love an iced tea," I said instead. Didn't want to scare the church ladies.

Molly handed me a Sharpie and a "Hello! My name is . . ." tag and then swept her gold lamé jumpsuit toward the mini-bar. I unleashed the Sharpie and filled in "Heidi" in the blank space, thinking of Micah in Black and wishing I knew how to draw a gnome, or at least a skull and crossbones.

"Hi," a voice behind me said.

I turned to see a woman with enormous green eyes and not a stitch of makeup. Frantic auburn curls were barely contained in a makeshift braid, tendrils framing a face dusted generously with freckles. She looked to be in her late forties; the auburn was sprinkled with unashamed strands of white. Her petite frame hid within a floor-length muumuu the color of burlap. Duck-billed Birkenstocks swallowed feet covered in wool socks. "Christened Barbara in 1959 by sweet but conformist parents. But you can call me Willow." She held out her hand, an arm stacked with Indian bangles toasting the gesture. "Had it legally changed during my commune days."

"I'm Heidi," I said, reaching for her hand. "I'm new." Molly approached and handed me a glass of iced tea before scuttling away to answer the doorbell.

"She's quite the woman," Barbara/Willow said, nodding after Molly, who'd already passed the water feature. I hoped she'd elaborate, but she only sipped slowly from a steaming Thermos she'd apparently brought with her. The logo on the mug read "Prairie Sun Co-op." I wondered what she was drinking. Parsnip chai? Maybe carrot wheatgrass tea?

Willow cocked her head to one side and asked, "So how many children do you have?"

"Just one," I said. "Nora. She's six months."

"A baby," Willow said, smiling appreciatively. "I have three. Hike's seventeen and a senior in high school, and the twins, Stream and Blue, are in middle school."

I gulped. "Holy mackerel," I said. "You must be exhausted permanently." And perhaps a fan of reefer to name your children after a day in the woods.

Willow laughed, smile lines creasing comfortably around her dancing eyes. "You know, it's really not that bad. I have some seriously chaotic days and some seriously great ones. It all evens out." She gestured around the room of chattering females. "This helps."

"How so?" I asked, crunching an ice cube and studying the star tattoo under her left ear.

Willow didn't have a chance to answer. Molly flitted into the room to announce we'd begin shortly in the den. I followed

Willow and the stream of women through the kitchen and down one step to a spacious family room lit by a crackling fire. Apple green suede couches and complimentary armchairs and otto-mans offered plenty of seating to our group of fifteen or so.

Molly sat on an oversize pillow on the floor in front of the fireplace. I shared a couch with Willow and a woman dressed in a collared shirt, cardigan, and slacks. Not khakis, these were definitely slacks. Her hair was pulled back into a severe French twist, completely out of harmony with an otherwise young face. She smiled nervously at me as she sipped hot tea from a china cup. I wondered if she'd brought her own formal dinner-ware like Willow had brought her hemp Thermos.

"Welcome, ladies," Molly began from her position on the floor. "I'm *thrilled* to have each of you in my home. Please join me in thanking God for our time together."

The room bowed its collective head as Molly took a deep breath, letting herself exhale slowly. "Jesus," she prayed, "I thank You for giving me the honor of knowing and loving these women. We want to serve You and love You better. Please help us get a step closer to that lofty goal in our next moments together. Amen."

The room murmured "amen" and waited in silence for Molly to continue.

"First," she said, looking at me, "I'd like to introduce you old-timers to a *brand new*-timer. Heidi Elliott is joining us for the first time. Heidi, why don't you introduce yourself and tell us a bit about what you do?"

Fifteen sets of eyes trained themselves on me, many of them smiling, some of them glazed over from an entire day of motherhood. I cleared my throat.

"I'm Heidi. My husband, Jake, and I have one child, a daughter named Nora." I stopped, considering whether or not it was appropriate to mention that this would be my only visit to their group, that I'd only come because I was scared of Molly and hacked at my husband, and to please not harass me any more when they saw me at First Lutheran. I continued, "I'm at home with Nora right now but will be resuming my work as a full-time Spanish teacher at Springdale High School after the holidays." I added quickly, "Thanks for letting me visit your group."

A murmur of welcome greeted the end of my little speech, and Molly smiled brilliantly, as if I had just finished reciting the Gettysburg Address for the first time all by myself.

"Wonderful," she said. "*Welcome*, Heidi. Now to business. As most of you know, we are beginning a new book this week. By popular vote, we've decided to work our way through this." She held up a small purple paperback with a single pink tulip on the front. "*Calm in the Storm: Mothering with a Quiet and Gentle Spirit*. I've ordered enough copies for all of us, so please pick one up on your way out." She set the book down, adding, "We'll discuss the first chapter next week."

A quiet and gentle spirit, eh? Not looking good for our hero, I thought, a wry smile escaping my lips. Not only did I feel neither quiet nor gentle, I had absolutely no desire to become that way. Watching grass grow would be fascinating in comparison to a quiet and gentle woman. Hadn't these women heard of Gloria Steinem?

"For tonight," Molly continued, "I thought we would spend a little time in the *luxury* of group prayer. So often we gloss right over this most important way to connect to each other and to God, so I'm pleased we have the *whole hour* to devote to praying with and for each other."

An hour to pray? Surely she jested. My all-time longest prayer had to have been during labor, and I dare say not all the words I used then would be, ahem, appropriate for these ears.

"Does that sound good to everyone?" Molly scanned the room. All the women looked suspiciously game, even Hempy Willow to my left and Laura Ingalls Wilder to my right. I tried my best to fake it and look pious, or at least pleasant.

"Before we pray, if you have anything on your heart for which you'd like prayer, please feel free to share with the group." Molly folded her hands on her lap, and the room went silent for a moment.

Laura Ingalls began. "I'd like to request prayer for my middle child, Elizabeth," she said, wringing her paper napkin in her hands. "We're having some discipline issues." She looked down at her lap, hesitant to elaborate.

A black woman sat on the chair next to Laura and wore a small gold necklace inscribed with the name Neesha. Meticulously rowed braids crowned her head and fell below her slender shoulders. Her beauty was striking, high cheekbones sloping toward a full mouth covered lightly in sheer gloss. She touched Laura's arm with long fingers, nails painted cherry red. "Do you want to give us any more details? It's perfectly fine if you don't. God doesn't need any more information, but it might make you feel better to share the burden."

We looked at Laura Ingalls Wilder, worried that her perfectly coiffed hair might become untidy should she start weeping. It looked like the dam was about to break.

"Um," Laura started, then stopped. "I think she's having sex!" she blurted, appalled immediately that she'd said the words. Her lip trembled dangerously, eyes filling with tears.

Neesha put her hand over Laura's. "Why do you think she's having sex?"

Laura dabbed at her eyes with her crumpled paper napkin. She gulped, steadying herself for confession. "She had her belly pierced last week without my consent, and," Laura closed her eyes, "she bought several of those cropped blouses that Whitney Spears wears."

Wrong name, but we got the point.

Laura shuddered, placing her hand to her white collar and fingering the cameo brooch she wore. Because I hadn't actually seen a woman wearing a brooch since the late eighties, I began to surmise the severity of piercings and exposed navels in the Ingalls Wilder home. This woman wouldn't last a day at Springdale High.

A rotund blonde woman in pink velour snorted from her place on an ottoman. She shook a head of curls and said, "Honey, I'd love to bare some midriff, but I'd worry about scaring small children." The room tittered with laughter, all eyes on Laura Ingalls to see if she liked midriff jokes. She did not.

"Does your daughter have a boyfriend?" asked a woman named Faith. Pin-straight black hair framed her face in a chin-length bob. She sat poised and elegant, dark eyes expressive behind Malcolm X frames.

"Not that I know of," Laura said, still fingering her brooch. "I haven't met anyone, at least."

Molly cleared her throat. "Other than the belly issue, then, there are no clear signs your daughter is sexually active?"

"Isn't that enough?" spewed Laura, then quickly gathered herself. "I just mean, there are *signs* one looks for as a mother, and I worry that Elizabeth is making some very poor choices."

Faith asked, "What does Elizabeth say when you discuss this with her?"

Laura looked like she'd been asked the question by Howard Stern. "We have not *discussed* this," she said haughtily. "I believe there are some things that are private and should *remain* so, no matter how cheapened they are by pervading culture." She spat the word "culture" as if to purge it from her mouth. "I have never discussed sex with my children other than when my husband and I explained the facts of life on their twelfth birthdays."

Boy, I bet that was a picnic, I thought. Bring the kids in from churning butter for a little chat about the birds and the bees from Mr. and Mrs. Repression.

Willow, who had until now kept her mouth shut, put down her co-op mug and looked squarely at Laura Ingalls. "You are her mother. Elizabeth must hear an authentic voice from her mother."

Laura looked surprised. She'd asked for prayer, after all, not two cents from Make Love Not War.

Willow continued, with soft eyes but a determined voice. "Your daughter is looking for you to respond to her behavior, which, for all intents and purposes, may very well be completely innocent. But she must know you love her and want God's best for her, including her body and her sexuality."

Laura gulped at the word "sexuality." This was not a woman who shops at Vicki's Secret, or even watches Oprah, for that matter.

"You must talk with her because you model Christ to her, and she must hear His voice above the din." With that, Willow sat back in her chair, took up her mug, and added softly, "We will pray for both of you." She looked at Laura with kindness and said, "It's a complicated thing, being a woman. You two need each other."

Laura seemed to be getting over the initial shock of Willow's words and began nodding slowly. She sat like that, nodding and thinking, for several moments, long enough for me to worry she might start rocking back and forth muttering things like, "Belly ring. Sex with boys. Oprah." Instead, she looked up, clear-eyed, and said, "Thank you."

Molly asked if anyone else had anything we could pray about. A woman with a name tag declaring "Katie" in loopy letters asked us to pray for her two-year-old, who had whooping cough, and Faith asked for prayer for her marriage, as she and her husband had very little time together lately. The big blonde asked us to pray for an increase in her patience, particularly with her mother-in-law, who had moved next door. I wondered if her mother-in-law thought midriff humor was funny, but judiciously kept this question to myself.

All prayer requests were offered without shame, and the listening women nodded with empathy, some of them jotting notes to themselves in calendars or journals.

Neesha led us in a quiet prayer, carefully giving voice to each woman's concern and asking God not only to resolve the conflicts but also to help the women respond with kindness toward themselves and their families. Neesha prayed with a confidence that someone was listening, which made me think she must do this sort of thing often. Laura Ingalls sniffed a lot and made good use of her napkin, rather nasty by now, but she kept it together and said "amen" with feeling at the end.

"Ladies," said Molly from her fireside perch, "feel free to linger and chat for as long as you'd like. Don't forget to pick up a book on your way out."

Some of the women rose and said their good-byes with smiles and hugs. Others continued chatting on ottomans and armchairs, evidently not in a hurry to return to their normal lives. I busied myself with my purse and empty tea glass so as not to invite any public displays of feminine affection. For a nonhugger, these moments were the most precarious.

Willow approached me after donning an enormous woven coat that could have been mistaken for a llama. "It was great to meet you, Heidi," she said. "I'll look for you Sunday, but we'll definitely see each other next week here."

"We'll see," I said. "I'll have to see about child care, and I'm really quite busy getting ready to go back to work."

Willow looked at me a moment, reading me like a page in her recycled newspaper. "Well, I hope it works out for you to come again. Like I said, a woman's life is complicated. We need each other." She smiled again, turned, and walked toward the door while pulling on a stocking hat complete with earflaps and chin tie.

I waved to Molly from across the room and headed quickly toward the door. A woman holding a cardboard box full of purple books handed me one of her charges. "Chapter One for next week," she chirped, already digging in the box for a book to give the woman behind me.

Closing my car door on the chilly evening, I sighed, tossed the book in my backseat, and headed for home, very thankful my house held one man and only one tiny female.

chapter/seven

I'd found that a babe of six months, while not able to boil water or answer the phone, could have an amazing ability to appreciate the finer points of interpretive dance. My own dancing prowess had been repeatedly scorned by the outside world, ridiculed by my best friend, and carefully ignored by every boyfriend from junior high onward.

Nora, however, truly recognized a master of movement when she saw one. So I didn't exactly move with any predictable rhythm. So I couldn't sing along and bust a move at the same time. Nora was able to look *beyond*. At last I had found a kindred spirit, a true Renaissance girl. At least until she reached sixth grade and wished me dead rather than do the Electric Slide in her presence.

It was late afternoon, prior to dinnertime mayhem, and Nora and I were boogying it up. Actually, I was doing most of the boogying, and she was watching me with keen interest from the couch. The last time we'd danced, I'd held her while we got our groove on, which had resulted in projectile vomiting halfway through the Bee Gees' "More Than a Woman." We were going for a less participatory role for Nora today.

It was my second time through "Thriller," and I was trying my best to reenact the video that had scarred me as a child, when the doorbell rang. I ran to turn down the music and opened the front door.

Ben leaned against our porch railing in a soft black corduroy shirt that matched long, giraffe eyelashes. My grandma would have called it a waste, such pretty eyes given to a man.

"Hi, Heidi," he said, brown eyes shining, his face still boasting the bronze of summer.

"Ben, come in," I said, holding the door open for him to step inside. He brushed me as he walked by. I blushed to realize I'd noticed.

"Nora," I called, "our friend Ben is here." Nora looked at Ben with my husband's blue eyes and offered a gummy grin.

"Hi, kiddo," Ben said. "You guys been cutting a rug in here? I heard MJ from halfway down the block." Ben looked at me, bemused.

"Actually, yes," I responded, not without a little huff in my voice. "Nora and I appreciate the many benefits of recreational dancing." I turned to my girl. "You don't care that Mommy looks like a convulsion in progress, do you, sweetheart?"

Ben laughed. "Now, don't be too hard on yourself, Heids. I recall a woman with more than enough confidence to overcome a noticeable lack of rhythm." His eyes crinkled with memory. "I found the end product absolutely endearing."

I smiled. "You're too kind, really." Really, he was. Ben danced like Astaire or Timberlake depending on the situation. Unlike most males in the universe, he was a joy to take to wedding receptions.

"Listen," he said, "I don't want to break up the dance party, but I have a favor to ask of you and your daughter."

"How can we help?" I asked, hefting Nora from her seat. "Need a hand moving heavy objects? Nora and I work out."

"It shows, particularly on Nora." He took her hand. "Is this wrist fat?"

"Worked hard to put that on her, buddy."

"I'm sure," Ben said, nodding and smiling. "No heavy lifting. I'm looking for something a bit unorthodox but far more valuable to me."

"Shoot," I said.

"Goossheee," agreed Nora. Such an articulate child.

"I'm wondering if you two might help me with an upcoming deadline," Ben said.

"How on earth can we help?" I asked, wary. "One of us is unable to operate a disposable camera without cussing, and the other isn't potty trained, making fieldwork a challenge."

Ben looked at me with a half smile, eyes taking in my whole face. "Heidi, you're very funny." Kept looking. "I'd forgotten how much I love your humor." Still looking, almost very awkward. "I've missed you."

Okay, definitely awkward. So why, then, did I love the compliment?

He cleared his throat. "I'd like to photograph you and Nora. My editor wants me to do a spread on American women in their work, both in and out of the home, and I would like you and Nora to be a part of it."

I squinted at him. "Is this a joke? Because women who have had children are notorious for becoming evil when victims of practical jokes, particularly when they involve cameras. I'm

just warning you." I pulled myself up to Pilates posture, sucking in my core for all it was worth.

"No joke," Ben said seriously. "I think you two, in many
ways, epitomize the beauty of the American female. You mother
Nora with such compassion, such caring, such humility." He
looked at me with the intensity that used to make my knees go
weak. Used to. "And yet you love her with humor, grace." He
smiled. "Barring Michael Jackson moments, that is."

I looked at Nora, unwilling to respond to his words or his
gaze. "And this peanut?" I asked. "I'm not sure Nora is the
cooperative subject you may be used to. She's no Gisele."

"Are you kidding?" Ben asked, eyes sparking. "*Far* more
beautiful." He drew his thumb down her cheek. "Pristine, soft
skin, the eyes, total trust in the camera. She's unspoiled. She's
perfect."

Well, that was true. But then again, I was her mother.

I looked out the front door to the cloudy fall day. Ben
waited.

"I'll do it," I said. "But only if you do your best to make
me look cute. A woman has her vanity, you know."

"Done," Ben said, grinning. "That will be the easiest
part."

He started for the door; Nora and I followed.

"I'll call you with the time and place," he said as he opened
the door. A periwinkle mist had covered the view from our
front porch, the setting sun obscured by clouds. "And thanks,
Heidi. I owe you."

"That's probably true, but I'll send you a modest bill," I
said, holding Nora close to me to keep her warm in the open
door.

"See you two," Ben said and bounded down the steps like a teenager.

"Your first photo shoot, sweet pea," I said as I closed the door. "I promise I won't become one of those psycho show business parents, relentlessly seeking the fame of her children."

With Nora back on the couch, I returned to the stereo. "Speaking of psycho show business types . . ." I said and cranked up "Thriller" one last time before dinner.

☙ ☙ ☙

By six thirty that evening, the mist outside had mushroomed into a full-blown downpour. A frigid November wind made the trees around our house creak and moan, their newly naked branches colliding in a sharp cacophony. I held Nora close to me while I stood by the window, watching for Jake's car. The streetlights bathed our quiet street in an eerie orange haze. The premature darkness of early winter unsettled me, and I fought off images of Jake's car in a ditch somewhere.

"Where's your papa?" I asked Nora, who was content in my arms, sucking the lifeblood out of an orange. She'd finished her dinner long ago and would be ready for her final hot toddy within the hour.

I walked to the kitchen counter and called Jake's number for the fifth time in the last thirty minutes. Right to voice mail. Where *was* he?

Nora was covered in suds and I was near calling the police when I heard Jake open the front door with his key. I stayed in the bathroom, both because I had an infant in the tub and because my relief that Jake was home was quickly melting into anger.

Jake stood in the doorway, his hair and clothes sopping wet.

I looked up from soapy Nora and said, "Where were you?"

Jake sighed, leaned up against the sink. "Hi, honey. My day was not so hot, thanks for asking."

"You've got to be kidding," I said, rinsing the last of the soap from Nora's slippery body. "I've been worried sick, have called you multiple times on your cell to no avail, and you want me to exchange pleasantries before I find out what the heck is going on? Jake, you're two hours late."

Jake ran his fingers through his hair. "I was helping some-one with car trouble." He watched me lift Nora out of the tub and opened her towel for the hand-off. Nora squirmed with delight to be tickled by her AWOL dad.

Someone with car trouble. My defenses lowered slightly, but, not quite ready to let Jake off the hook, I asked, "Why didn't you answer your phone?"

Jake and Nora headed toward the nursery. "The battery must be dead. I'm sorry, Heidi, I really am. Helping seemed the right thing to do, and I didn't realize until I saw the look on your face that I should have made sure to call."

I took Nora from Jake's arms and finished drying her off. I supported her neck with my hand and lowered her pinky clean rolls to the rug. She watched me from below as I put on a fresh diaper. "It's okay," I said, fishing with one hand for clean paja-mas in Nora's bottom drawer. "I just become a neurotic spouse when you don't call, Jake. I see limbs and shattered glass and a host of other images from *Dateline*." I turned, handing him our bathed, clothed, lavender-smelling daughter. "We just need a 'this is why I'm late' call, right, Nora?"

Jake kissed her on both cheeks, me on the lips, and said, "I'm sorry. I promise not to let it get to *Dateline* status again."

I could scarcely believe him, as this was not the first time calls had gone unanswered, all in the name of noble causes and legitimate excuses. But he was extremely good with our daughter, and I found him sexually attractive, so what was a girl to do?

Jake put Nora to bed with a reserve bottle while I heated up our dinner. He kissed me again when he came to the table, his repentance full-force after cuddling with Nora for a while. She had a way of causing him to rearrange his priorities. We sat down and Jake blessed the meal. This particular supper, my classic lasagna with a crisp salad and a fresh loaf of focaccia, needed less blessing than others, but I played along.

"So, other than rescuing a stranded traveler, how was your day?" I asked, savoring the warm pasta and my first sip of wine.

"Fine," Jake replied, his mouth full. "Long. It probably wouldn't have been quite as long if Jana's car hadn't broken down, but it was still a rough one."

Jana? "You mean you were rescuing Jana Van Fleet?" I kept eating, finding it to be a safe response for the moment.

"Yeah, didn't I say that?" Jake asked, buttering a big wedge of bread. "When we finished our meeting, her car wouldn't start, so I tried jumping it with my cables. Even though the thing had to have cost at least eighty grand, it would not start.

After working on it for a good forty-five minutes, we gave up and I gave her a lift to her house."

I patted my mouth with my napkin. "Wasn't Rob there to take her home?" Rob was Jake's right-hand man, second in command at the shop and a loyal friend.

"Rob had to get home to Samantha and the kids," Jake said, glossing over the irony of that statement. "It was just as quick for me to take her home."

I suddenly felt too tired to move, much too tired to talk. I pushed my fork around my plate, quietly mourning my lost appetite and a good piece of lasagna that would have to wait for a microwave and tomorrow's lunch. Jana Van Fleet, knockout heiress, in Jake's car and at her home alone with my husband during a rainstorm. My visual picture abruptly shifted from *Dateline* and crumpled Toyotas to steamy car windows, a Tudor mansion, cozy fireplace, two people laughing as they dried out after a downpour. Shut it off! I screamed to my inner remote, which defiantly disobeyed.

"You know, Jake," I said wearily, "I'm exhausted. I think I'll turn in early tonight, maybe read in bed for a while." I carried my full plate and glass to the kitchen. "You can just leave the dishes in the sink. I'll do them in the morning."

I slumped toward the kitchen. "I'm sorry I snapped at you when you got home, Jake. Nora and I are both really glad you're okay." Without looking him in the eye, I turned toward our bedroom.

"Heidi," Jake called after me. "Is everything okay? Do you want to talk about anything?"

No, please, no talking. I blinked back tears, probably from exhaustion. "I'm okay. Just tired."

I slipped into my pj's without turning on the light and crawled between the sheets. My body felt like lead, my eyes weighted. I rolled onto my side and hugged an extra pillow. A fleeting memory registered in my head that I hadn't said a word to my husband about Ben's visit. Tomorrow, I thought, right before falling hard into a dark and dreamless sleep.

℮ ℑ ℮

From eons away, I heard Nora's cries on the baby monitor. With the willpower of Richard Simmons, I propped my eyes open, squinting to focus on the digital clock.

Seven thirty.

Jake was long gone, having opened the store for the ridiculous working hours of a painter. Nora was crying and sounded like she had been for a while. I wondered how long I'd slept through her wailing.

Using my hands to push myself up, I rose slowly to a sitting position, moaning as I went. My head felt the size and shape of a watermelon. My flannel pajamas felt prickly. When I tried swallowing, my throat screamed, Never do that again! I pulled myself out of bed, fumbling as I put on my robe. Just when I was about to wrap a down quilt around my shivering shoulders, I felt instead like turning on the air conditioner, no matter that it was November and couldn't have been above forty degrees at that hour. I compromised by dragging the quilt behind me, ready for the next breakdown of my internal thermostat.

Nora greeted me with her own runny nose and temperature. I nursed her, trying very hard to concentrate on not letting go of my daughter, who seemed to have gained at least sixty-five pounds overnight and ran the risk of rolling out of my Jell-O arms and across the floor like a bowling ball. Nora finished a frantic and uncomfortable meal, and we two sickies padded to the kitchen for a bland breakfast of butter on toast for me and three Cheerios for her.

"I think you need to come home," I said into the phone, my voice sounding like Darth Vader's. "Nora and I are sick." I could hear some customers shooting the jive in the background as Jake listened to my growls.

"Honey, I can't . . . uh, leave the store . . . this morning," he replied, his speech fragmented. He muttered numbers to himself; I could hear him clicking away on his computer.

"Jake, I can barely move, and Nora is a fountain of snot," I whined. "Isn't there anyone who can cover for you?"

"I'm sorry, Heids," he said, muffled again. "Fall sale begins today and we're already understaffed as it is. Can't you call Lauren or something?"

I imagined Lauren pulling up in a candy striper uniform, consulting her training as an EMT (the youngest on the force), singing previously unreleased Celtic lullabies as she nursed Nora and me back to health. Puke.

"I'll think of something," I said, wanting only a nap and the irresponsibility of my life before Nora. Wasn't there a time when I could just *be* sick because I was?

"I'll pray for you two, hon," Jake said.

Sweet, but how about something a little more hands-on?

We hung up and I shuffled with Nora to our bed. We burrowed under the covers and within two minutes fell into an achy slumber.

℮ ഉ ℮

Not a half hour later, Nora awoke, screaming. My left arm had fallen asleep under her weight. Her nose and eyes were full of gunk, and she was warm. I tried to comfort her, wishing she was old enough to learn phlegm management skills. Poor baby needed help but didn't know how to ask. I rocked her on the edge of our bed, saying over and over, "Mommy's here, sweet pea. We'll feel better soon."

I fought through my mental fog, trying to remember how to be a responsible parent of a sick kid. It came to me: We needed drugs.

I rifled through our packed medicine cabinet and located a dark blue tub of Vicks, smearing some on Nora's little chest and adding a dollop to my own for good measure. Nora's nose wrinkled at the waft of menthol. I closed my eyes, thrown back to the healing effects of my own mom smearing blue goop under my stuffy nose.

After reading the label six times and calling the pediatrician, I finally felt comfortable with giving Nora a dose of infant Tylenol. Though fearful even in optimum conditions of overdosing my child, my present cloudy mental state made me even more paranoid of giving Nora the dosage for a beluga whale.

How do people do this? I lamented, rocking Nora in her room while trying to keep my snot from dripping on her hot little head. I have only one child, who's really a rather nice child, and I can barely keep my head above water. What would I do if I had two, three, four kids who were sick at the same time?

I rocked and pouted, pouted and rocked.

These things happen, I barked to my wimpy self. Think of pioneer women! Think of huge Irish Catholic families! Think of anyone other than yourself, you big ninny!

My pep talk failed miserably. I wished for the luxury of weeping bitterly into my pillow before succumbing to sleep. Judging by the way Nora was clinging to the veins in my neck, I might as well have wished for peace in the Middle East.

And it was only nine o'clock.

Just then, the phone rang. After deliberating whether or not to move and risk expending all that valuable energy on a telemarketer, I creaked to my feet and made my way toward the family room with Nora in my arms.

"Hello?" I croaked.

"Heidi, is that *you*?" a bubbly female voice greeted me.

"May I ask who's calling?"

"It's Molly Langdon, dear. I was just calling to *thank* you for coming to our little get-together this last Wednesday. You were *such* a delight to have, and I *do* hope to see you again this week."

I blew my nose away from the phone, scaring the wits out of Nora. "Molly," I said over Nora's sobs, "thanks for your call, but this is really not a good time. Could I call you back?"

"My good gracious, Heidi," Molly exclaimed. "You sound absolutely *horrendous*. And is that Nora? Poor *things*. What are your symptoms?"

I rasped, "Um, raging sore throat, flooding nose, headache, fever. The usual winter cold, I guess." I used the last Kleenex in the box on Nora's red nose.

"Don't you worry," Molly said, completely resolved about something that would probably make me nervous. "We are *perfectly* prepared for days like this. I'll have someone over within the hour."

"What?" I gasped. "Molly, my house is a disaster and I can barely see out of my puffy eyes. I promise I'll come to your group again, but *please* don't send anyone over here."

Ignoring my jabber, Molly interjected, "Heidi, *listen* to me." She suddenly sounded like someone with a lot of authority, so I listened. "You are in *no* condition to be taking care of Nora or anyone else today, including yourself. We have a rotating list in Moms' Group for emergencies, and I'm sending someone over to get you two feeling better." Her tone softened. "Dear, we have *all* been where you are. And you cannot do this alone without being completely *miserable*."

She had a point.

"Someone will be over by ten. Until then, just try to rest and keep Nora relatively comfortable. *Help is on the way*."

With that, she hung up, and I stared blankly at the receiver. I reached over to place it back on the cradle and sat down in an armchair with a groan. Nora looked up at me, sniffing, and seemed to say, It's about time someone made a good decision around here.

I was not in any shape to argue with an infant wise beyond her months. Nora nuzzled her runny nose into my neck. Entwined like a congested pretzel, we hunkered down to wait for our guest.

chapter/eight

Through my fog, I heard a soft knock on the front door and then the creak of someone letting herself in. I tried with Herculean strength to get out of bed, where I'd been snoozing while Nora napped in her crib.

I failed.

A thought flickered through my pounding head that if the person in our house was a burglar here to steal my most precious earthly possessions, I hoped the noise would be kept to a bare minimum. Unable to fight it off, I drifted in and out of an uncomfortable sleep until waking enough to see a face peeping into my bedroom.

"Hi," I said. "Come in, please."

The door opened a bit, and I saw the full form of my own personal Mary Poppins. It was Willow. This time her wild hair was pulled back and held in place with two chopsticks. She smiled. "Hi, Heidi," she said in a well-versed inside voice that said, I don't want to wake a sleeping child. I loved her.

"Thank you so much for coming over," I started to say, but was interrupted by a sneeze. Not a very dainty one, either.

"You're very welcome," she said, bringing me a fresh box of tissues. "How are you feeling?"

I closed my eyes. "Like molasses with a five-star headache."

She stood at the foot of my bed with her arms folded. "When's the last time you took some Tylenol or ibuprofen?"

"Um," I said, furrowing my brow, "I'm not sure if I've taken any yet. I gave some to Nora. . . ." My voice faded. What was the question?

"Okay," Willow said, patting my leg through the down comforter. "I'll be right back with some medicine and a glass of water. You just relax." She disappeared from sight for a few minutes while I looked intently at the insides of my eyelids.

"Take two of these," she commanded when she returned, handing me Tylenol and nearly a gallon of water. I obeyed. "You should finish this jug as soon as you can. We're going to flush this bug right out of your system." She put the water on my bedside table, between Kleenex and Vicks.

Willow placed a cool hand across my forehead. "You're a bit warm, but the acetaminophen should take care of that. Go to sleep and don't worry about Nora. I've done this many times." She started for the door, turning off lamps as she went.

"Willow," I said weakly. "Are you going to get fired from your job because you're caring for the less fortunate?"

She smiled. "I'm the boss of me, so no firing. I run a small art gallery close to downtown. I called in one of my college girls to cover for me this afternoon."

"Kids?"

"Hike drives to school himself. He'll pick up the twins and get them home. I left an eggplant and feta pizza for them for dinner. They're good kids. I know they'll be fine without me."

"Husband?" I asked, knowing they function basically like extra children.

"Passed away six months ago," she said softly, her eyes clouding a bit.

My stomach dropped. "I'm so sorry."

"We'll talk about that some other time. You just worry about yourself and getting better so you can resume your chaotic life." She smiled, her hand on the doorknob. "Nora'll be driving herself home and eating a pizza for dinner before you know it. You don't want to miss too much." Willow backed into the hallway and shut the door without a sound.

I let my head fall like dead weight onto my pillow. A woman in mourning is nursing me and my daughter back to health, I thought. I met her less than a week ago.

My body began to relax, careening slowly toward a hard sleep. I thought of Jake's promise to pray. Before succumbing to slumber, I shot this heavenward: Very timely response. I owe You one.

ℰ ℈ ℰ

When I woke, it was dark outside, and our house brimmed to overflowing with the smell of good food. I pulled a deep breath through newly cleared nostrils, and my empty stomach growled a fierce response. I extricated arms and legs from a tangle of sheets and sat on the edge of my bed, waiting for the clarity that eventually comes with wakefulness.

In a moment, Willow came to mind, and I remembered being saved by her good works. My body had started to feel more like a human being's and less like Dorothy's in a Kansas tornado. The ache was gone; only weakness remained.

I shuffled into the kitchen in my bathrobe and found Willow singing in a rich alto to my daughter, who watched her with delight from her perch in the high chair. Nora was eating pieces of peaches and grapes and looked much more like my little girl than she had that morning.

"Hi," I said, suddenly feeling shy. I ran my fingers through my snarled hair, wondering how Willow felt about Chia Pets. "It smells amazing in here."

Willow continued emptying the nectar of the gods from my food processor and took stock of the woman standing before her. "Good," she pronounced. "You have color in your face again. Sit down and I'll bring you a glass of water."

"I'll get it," I said, starting for the cupboard to retrieve a glass.

I thought Willow was going to drop-kick me as she stepped in my path. The woman had catlike reflexes. "Sit down, please, before I have to get violent. You may not think it looking at me, but I take tae kwon do, and I'm pretty good." She arched one eyebrow. "Sit."

I sat, and took from her another twenty-four ounces of water. This Willow person took hydration to a whole new level. After a few gulps, I said, "I cannot possibly thank you enough for coming to my rescue. I'm not sure what I would have done."

She smiled and dropped some pasta into a stockpot of boiling water. "You would have done fine, but it might have taken you a few extra days to feel as good as you do now." She tasted the sauce, closing her eyes for full effect, and added some garlic and a dash of olive oil.

"Did you have this kind of angel rescue league when your kids were little?" I asked.

"I probably could have found help, but I wasn't very good at asking for it," she replied flatly. She looked up from her work and said, "Michael's illness taught me many lessons, but the biggest was probably the ability to ask for help." Her eyes teared as she turned back to the sauce.

"I'm so sorry for your loss," I offered feebly, my words empty, empty, empty. "If you don't mind my asking, how did your husband die?"

"He had ALS, Lou Gehrig's disease," Willow said, taking out a cutting board to start slicing a baguette. "It's an illness that basically drains the body of its strength and self-sufficiency over a period of years. There is no cure, and the only treatments merely ease the pain of dying." Willow was really sawing away at that bread; I wondered if we should continue this conversation when she wasn't armed with a serrated weapon.

I swallowed. "I can't even imagine. How did you survive?" I moved toward Nora, who had inhaled all her fruit and was hunting around for more in the crevices of her chair.

"Grace," she said, starting to butter each piece of bread. I could see her smiling to herself. "It still strikes me as odd that I could even identify grace in the last few years, but it's true. At the beginning of Michael's illness, before he'd lost any real mobility and when his speech was slowing but still understandable, I remember reading Scripture with him one night before bed." She stopped and took a big breath. "We read the passage in 2 Corinthians 12 where God assures us His grace is sufficient for us."

I waited as she wrapped the loaf of bread in foil and tucked it into the oven.

Willow stood up, a potholder in each hand, and looked at me. "*Sufficient* grace. Not an excess, not a scarcity, but sufficient for us. I cannot tell you how many times I clung to that promise throughout the next months and years."

I turned away, unable to hold Willow's gaze. Her eyes reflected deep sorrow and faith at the same time, and I found I didn't have a whole lot to say about either one. I knew I had never walked through anything near what she had, and I was positive I couldn't have responded with her dignity and trust. I kept my eyes on Nora, afraid the look on my face would betray the shock I felt at her words.

"So," Willow continued, moving toward the stove again, "I survived with God's grace, which came in many unexpected forms." She took the pot of pasta off the stove and brought it to a colander waiting in the sink. "For example," she said through the billowing steam, "the Moms' Group was very creative in their hospitality, just like James tells us to be."

Who's James? I thought, wisely biting my tongue until I realized she was talking about the Bible again.

"People helped out in all sorts of ways. Molly Langdon picked up, washed, and folded our laundry every Saturday for two and a half years. Jenna Bailey organized the meal brigade, which provided us with three hot meals every week. Sara Gutierrez and Neesha Jackson took turns coming to our house to clean it, top to bottom, every Monday without fail."

Willow shook her head as she remembered. "And that was just the Moms' Group. Others organized pancake breakfasts, benefit runs for ALS research, a memorial fund in Michael's honor. One anonymous donor from our church made a sizable contribution to the boys' college funds. Because of that one person, I won't have to worry about how to pay to send Hike to school next year."

She scurried out of the kitchen with placemats I hadn't used since Thanksgiving 1994. After setting the table for two, she returned and said, "And there was an entire army of people praying their socks off for Michael's healing, for our sanity, for our health as we cared for him. I'm sure they covered it all because God certainly showed Himself to be in the details."

"But weren't you angry?" I blurted, cutting through the sugary talk.

"Of course," Willow said with a shrug. "I still have angry days. This is not the life I chose, I argue with God." She looked out the kitchen window, quiet. After a moment she spoke slowly. "It's horrible to kiss your husband and know he won't always be able to respond. Every time we made love I wondered if it was the last time, and soon it was. I'd watch him with our boys and weep angrily, alone, knowing they were being robbed of their father." Her voice had become darker, but she was not complaining, which, in my estimation, was a feat of unparalleled strength.

"Heidi," she said, looking at me as she spoke, "I will never know all the reasons why Michael had to suffer the way he did or why we had to suffer along with him. But I can make sense of this by knowing, more today than three years ago, that the God I serve loves me with a stubborn, ferocious love and wants nothing more than for me to draw near Him."

She watched my face and must have seen the skepticism I was trying to mask. "I know," she said, almost chuckling. "I never would have believed that, either. I can only assure you I know it's true. Michael knew it, too, which is still a great comfort. He knew when he died he'd get to meet the One who loves him even more than I, which is really saying something considering how I loved that man." At this, her voice finally broke, and she stood in my kitchen, soft, silent tears streaming down her face.

I waited, remembering all those huggy people at Molly's house and feeling the disturbing impulse to do the same. As I was virally compromised, I merely handed her a Kleenex from the box I clutched.

"Thank you," she mumbled, covering her face with the tissue. "I miss him so much." Willow smiled a lopsided, I've-just-been-crying smile. "Kiss Jake like a honeymooner when he gets home, okay?"

She moved again to the dining room, finished setting the table, and returned a few minutes later in coat and gloves. "You're all set," she said, gesturing to the stove. "Pasta's ready. Just spoon on the sauce when you're ready to eat. Bread's keeping warm in the oven, and there's a salad covered in the fridge. I made a chocolate cake," she said, pointing to a cake dome on the buffet in the dining room, "and left some hazel-nut roast by your coffeemaker. It's Chilean and organic."

I rose from my chair and hugged myself through my terry-cloth tent. "Thank you," I said. "I don't know what to say, Willow."

She smiled at me and touched my cheek. "You are welcome. I know very well what it means to need a little help. It's my absolute joy to be on this side of the equation."

Willow kissed Nora on her head and talked with her in her ear. I hoped she was giving her the recipe for the chocolate cake, which was already making me drool from a room away.

Then Willow beckoned me toward her and Nora. "May I pray with you girls before I go?"

"Yes," I said, knowing she could have asked me to do an Irish jig or the "Hokey Pokey" in that moment and I would have sweetly complied.

"Father," Willow prayed, "I thank You for Your grace sufficient. We heavily rely on it, and You never fail. I ask You to bathe this home in peace and healing, giving all three of the Elliotts a good night's rest and renewed health in the morning. You are so good to us, Lord. We love and thank You. In Jesus' name, Amen."

Willow squeezed my hand, tucked an orange wool scarf inside her llama coat, smooched Nora, and was gone. Just like that. My first Mary Poppins experience and I hadn't even made it out of my bathrobe.

I had a feeling that was the point.

℮ ℈ ℮

"Jake, you would not have believed this woman," I said, nearly shoveling penne into my mouth with my fork. We'd put Nora to bed early. Shortly after Willow's departure, my child had plummeted from her pleasant, recuperative state and had begun what ended up being a full hour of nonstop whining.

She'd thrashed and gnashed about an early bedtime and griped about how undemocratic we were being, but she finally closed red-rimmed eyes and gave in to sleep.

Jake looked like he was thoroughly enjoying Willow's Pasta of Love, probably thanking his lucky stars she'd intervened before we had to resort to ramen noodles and frozen waffles. From salad onward, the meal tasted like happiness on wheels. Garlic-infused butter from the toasted sourdough dripped happily from Jake's chin.

He chewed thoughtfully. "I'm trying to place her. Her name is actually Willow? Who's her husband?"

"His name was Michael. He passed away last year from ALS," I said, launching into the background info. Retelling Willow's story to Jake did not make it any easier to digest. Indeed, relating their hardship to my own perfectly healthy husband made the depth of Willow's sorrow even more overwhelming.

I searched Jake's face as I spoke, its details, lines, and freckles suddenly, urgently important to commit to memory. He listened without comment, intermittently looking at me with big, sorrowful eyes, moved by Willow and Michael's story and by the open kindness shown to his girls that afternoon.

We finished the rest of the meal quietly, commenting every now and then on mundane matters like the hectic sale day at Jake's store and the chilly weather forecast. Jake and I helped ourselves to gargantuan slices of Willow's chocolate cake, taking turns rolling our eyes into the backs of our heads. This cake, as Annie would say, was so good it could make a woman slap her own grandma. And I had one sweet grandma.

"I'll get this recipe from Willow," I said, using the tines of my fork to pick up every remaining crumb. "In fact, I might consider serving only this chocolate cake for every meal until spring. Annie would kill me, but you'd love me large, wouldn't you, honey?"

Jake was watching my face intently, clearly not thinking about the cake, for which I pitied him. "Heids," he said, "I think you should go back to that Moms' Group this week. I've been praying about it."

I laid down my fork, smoothed my napkin. "Since when do you *pray* about *my* decisions?"

"Since last summer when I started praying, period," Jake replied with a soft look on his face.

I remembered him telling me that last summer had been an important one for him spiritually, but to be frank I'd had no idea what to ask or say about it, so I'd said nothing. It was around that time that Jake had begun keeping his Bible on his nightstand and reading it every morning. Come to think of it, he'd also been much less inclined to skip church, even during football season. Still, it hadn't occurred to me that his Bible phase had much to do with me.

I piled my silverware on my plate and pushed back my chair. "Well, thanks for thinking of me, but I've got it covered." I stood up from the table.

Jake put his hand out to stop me. "Heidi, I'm not going to push this. You're a big girl, and I know you are very capable of making adult decisions."

I let the "big girl" part slide, trying to concentrate on the larger picture here.

"But I really hope you'll go to Molly's group again," Jake said, his shoulders slumping. "Molly, Willow, the others—I think they would be great friends and mentors." He stopped, measuring his words. "And they know Jesus well. We can't teach Nora to love God if we don't know who He is."

Jake cocked his head and looked through the dining room window to our backyard, pitch black but for the luminous shadow cast by a streetlight. I watched his face, weighing his words.

"I'll go," I conceded. "For you, I'll go. For Willow's kindness, I'll go."

Jake's gaze left the backyard and returned to my face. He smiled, took my hand.

"But," I added, cautioning him, "don't expect me to be who I'm not, Jake. I'm not a Bible beater, and I never will be. I feel nothing when I pray. And I sure as heck don't know how Willow went through hell and didn't curse God for it."

I sighed, feeling the weight of my questions. "But I'll go to that darn group and listen to what they have to say."

Jake pulled me onto his lap, and I nuzzled my face under his jawbone. Scratchy whiskers, in full bloom at this hour, sandpapered my skin, but I just inhaled deeply the clean, honest, hard-working smell of my husband.

"You *are* awfully nice, you know," I said into his neck.

"I really am," he said, arms wrapped around me, fingers tracing slow patterns on my back.

"If I can get as nice as you by keeping my Bible by my pillow, Moms' Group is worth a shot, right?" I kissed his neck.

He pulled away and looked at me, eyes twinkling. "You'd have to open it once or twice, too, heathen."

"Watch it, Billy Graham," I said, kissing his lips. Just like a honeymooner.

chapter/nine

"Just please don't let them sing," Annie arched her eyebrows at me over her reading glasses. She continued perusing the menu, looking nothing like a dentist in her wraparound black dress with knee-high Italian leather boots and the turquoise necklace I'd given her a few moments ago.

"I can't promise anything," I said with a shrug, knowing perfectly well there were no singing waiters in this restaurant.

Sophie's Café had the best crepes in town and a killer chocolate soufflé, but was still friendly and casual enough to serve a seven-month-old without upturned noses and dramatic sighs. Sophie and Max Rosenberg, the restaurant's owners, had converted an old general store on Main Street, polishing up the antique tin ceiling tiles and refinishing the old pine floor. Walls and fabrics warmed the large dining room in apple green, cranberry, and curry. I sipped my water with lime, feeling smug with my choice for the birthday luncheon locale.

Taking off her glasses and closing her menu, Annie made faces with Nora, who squealed in delight. I wasn't sure if squealing fit with Sophie's ambiance but decided to let it go for birthday girl entertainment purposes.

"So tell me: How does thirty feel?" I closed my menu, having decided on the crab cakes with an order of tomato bisque. I hoped the soup would shake off some of the cold of early December; my hands were still ice even after having ten minutes to thaw.

Annie finished "This Little Piggy" with Nora's hand and sat back in her chair. She sighed with the drama of Joan Rivers. "Thirty feels like lemon juice in a paper cut. Fingernails on a chalkboard. The proverbial kick in the pants."

"Annie, please," I said, getting Nora's bottle ready. It was her lunchtime, too, and in lieu of whipping it out in Sophie's storage closet, I'd pumped before leaving the house. Even enduring the bovine experience of being sucked dry by a machine was worth it to enjoy lunch with my best friend.

"Do you really feel that bad about it?" I asked, lifting Nora out of the high chair and cradling her in my arms. She made a rather vocal show of enjoying the first few gulps of milk, but I couldn't fault her as I felt the same way about my upcoming crab cakes.

"Oh, you know," Annie said, dismissing the whole day with a wave of her hand. "I'm as happy as one can be in my position, I guess. I'm financially comfortable, in good health, have great friends. However, and I regret to mention such petty details, I have no one to spend my life with, no one to kiss me on my birthday morning, and no one with whom to share a burial plot. No kids, no husband, not even a boyfriend." She took a pull of her ice water as if it were Schlitz from the can. "But I do have money, molars, and marathons, so why complain? I'm a happy, fulfilled, thirty-year-old spinster."

"At least you're seeing the glass half-full," I said, mopping up Nora's milk mustache before putting her on my shoulder to burp. "You always were such a Pollyanna."

"Listen, sister," Annie said with a scowl, "don't sit there with your beautiful baby girl and the rock on your left hand and tell me about glasses being half-full. People with perfect lives don't mind turning thirty."

"My life is not perfect," I said, "and it's not a rock. It might even be a cubic zirconia, for all I know. Jake is not a man of means."

Nora let a rumbling, masculine belch escape her and then said something like, "Woo-hoo!" I put her back into eating position, mildly chagrined that my daughter sounded like she watched a lot of monster truck rallies and Hulk Hogan reruns.

Our server, a pleasantly plump brunette named Madge, came to get our order, first taking a few moments to swoon over Nora, who closed her eyes and tightened her straight-jacket grip on the bottle. I asked for the soup and cakes, and Annie ordered the chicken Florentine crepes. We agreed with Madge that these items would serve as a warm-up to two chocolate soufflés. Whisking away our menus, Madge gave us a perfunctory nod and Nora a pat on the head before scurrying away.

"You look beautiful, Annie," I said appreciatively. "I'm serious. You look more beautiful today than any birthday before this one. Excluding, perhaps, your sweet sixteenth, which we planned for months and on which you woke up with a raging rash all over your face caused by an overnight avocado mask." I giggled. "The rash that complicated the wooing of Marc

Struthers at your first boy-girl party, even with spin the bottle and the built-in advantage of adolescent male hormones."

Annie winced. "I don't know what was worse: the rash or Marc Struthers." She swirled her water with a cocktail straw. "He's gay, you know. Gay or married, I can't remember. I just remember he was definitively crossed off the list for a viable reason, not that the rash incident left anything unresolved between us."

I chuckled and lifted Nora up to my shoulder for her last burp. This one was dainty, more befitting of a ladies' luncheon at a crepe-selling café. Her body relaxed completely in my arms, slumped atop my shoulder like a twenty-pound lump of brown sugar. I loved the post-meal moments when my daughter, warm and cuddly, laid her heavy head on me and bore striking, contented resemblance to Buddha, except of the Western European persuasion.

Madge returned, bearing plates of artfully presented food. I returned Nora to the high chair and opened a packet of Club crackers. Nora grabbed one, taking turns gnawing on it with toothless gums and staring at its alien form. We were still in the stage when salt was surprising.

Sophie's was in full swing of the lunchtime shift. The room vibrated with the rhythm of relaxed conversation. My soup burst with flavor and warmth, and I told Madge the crab cakes were perfect.

"Shells his own every morning, real early," she said, I supposed referring to Max. She filled my water glass, looking over her bifocals as if to scan the room for informants. "If you ask me," she said in lowered voice, "imitation would work just as well." She arched her brows at me and scuttled away.

Judging by her editorial comments, I imagined the Rosenbergs had also received Madge's recommendations for waxy sundae cherries and Bac-O-Bits.

I asked Annie about her crepes, but she ignored me. Annie's chair faced the café's entrance, and she was staring as the door swung shut on a newly arrived party. I turned my head toward the door and gulped.

"You have got to be kidding me," Annie muttered, dragging her eyes from the door and narrowing her gaze on me. "Isn't that Ben?"

I looked at her blankly.

Her eyes widened. "You knew he was in town?"

"I can't believe I forgot to tell you," I confessed, remembering, too, that Jake had not yet been told about our plans for a photo shoot. "He's back on assignment, he says to stay. I guess he bought that bungalow for sale on Hollowbrook, pretty close to us."

"Heidi," Annie whispered loudly, "*how* could this escape your notice when talking to your *best friend*? Ex-boyfriend moves in practically next door and you *neglect* to mention it?" She leaned toward me, eyes big. "And I even reminisced about Marc Struthers, for Pete's sake! Didn't that ring any bells?"

I looked at her sheepishly, taking a timid bite of a crab cake. "I'm really sorry, Annie. I innocently forgot, I promise."

"How long have you known?" Annie asked, cutting into her crepe with vigor.

Ben was sauntering toward our table with a wide grin.

"He's coming," I said, taking a drink of water to swish out any wayward food particles.

"Well, this picture is certainly a blast from my past," Ben said. "Hi, Heidi. Hello, Nora," he said, touching her cheek. Nora slurped up wet cracker in response.

"And Annie," Ben said, taking in the birthday girl with a long glance. "It's great to see you. Wow, you look amazing."

"Hi, Ben," Annie said, fingering her new necklace. "It's great to see you, too. It's been a very long time. I didn't even know you were back in town."

Ben leaned one arm on the back of Nora's chair. "Yeah, back in good old Springdale. I'm shooting some pieces around here, traveling a bit. And I hear you're fixing teeth. What a pair of professional women: a dentist and a teacher. You guys cleaned up good."

"Ben," I interjected into the reunion schmooze, "congratulate Annie. It's her thirtieth birthday today. We're celebrating."

"Congrats, Annie," Ben said with a sly grin. "As I recall, you were always the first to fall in the birthday category. I'm not 'til March, and Heidi, aren't you in January?"

"May, actually," I said, irked that I'd remembered the exact date of Ben's birth but he couldn't even remember the month of mine.

"Right," Ben said, looking at Annie and smiling mischievously. "Well, I know when a man's not wanted. I'll let you girls celebrate. Happy birthday, Annie. Thirty becomes you." He smiled and returned to his dining partner, a suit with salt and pepper hair and tortoiseshell frames whom I guessed to be one of Ben's editors.

"Unbelievable," Annie said, her cheeks flushed. "He's still an uncontrollable flirt, after all these years." She shook her head and took a bite of her crepes. "He does look good, though, doesn't he?"

"I suppose," I said with feigned indifference. "I'm beginning to suspect he spray tans. No one's that ruddy in December."

Annie shrugged. "He travels, probably to places where the sun shines more than four months out of the year." She drew her hair into a loose knot with her hands, then let it fall unharnessed down her back. "Anyway, the fact remains that you didn't tell me you'd seen him and that he's back in Springdale. What's going on? You've been known to describe to me, in great detail, the condition of your postpartum hemorrhoids. But no dish on the ex-boyfriend? I don't get it."

I gave Madge the high sign from across the room. I hoped my look said, "Chocolate soufflé, and please hurry." Nora was nearing nap time, and I could almost feel my minutes cascading through the hourglass. I looked at Annie. "I haven't told you the whole story."

Annie waited, her face revealing her skepticism. Even with his charm and strings of compliments, she'd never trusted Ben farther than she could throw him or his Nikon.

"I'm going to be in a photo shoot for him. With Nora. Something about the beauty of contemporary American women." I watched her for a reaction.

Annie put down her fork and lined it up with the rest of her flatware, taking care to make each item equidistant from the next. The woman was a dentist, remember, even in knee-high black boots.

She cleared her throat and looked across the table at me. "Heidi, you know I am cautious, to say the least, about Ben and his intentions. Maybe he's changed since high school and college; Lord knows I have. And I'm sure a photo shoot is very commonplace for him and maybe even innocent."

I waited. "But . . . ?"

"But I just want you to be careful. You have a lot to be careful for." She was looking at Nora; I was looking at my wedding band.

"I know and I will," I said, newly determined to say something about this whole thing to Jake. "You know Ben means nothing to me, right, Annie?"

She smiled. "I know you are the greatest friend a girl could find and an amazing wife and mother. But I also know you are a human being and that old habits die hard, that's all."

Madge arrived with our chocolate, for which I gave her my most endearing smile. She smirked, apparently having seen the Chocolate Smile before and knowing it wasn't really meant for her.

I sank my teeth into the first warm mouthful, thanking God for the French man or woman who had invented this sublime pleasure and had made my life such a happy one. I dipped my pinky into the lava, cooled it a bit, and slipped some into Nora's mouth.

She shared my bliss. Atta girl.

"Did you hear me?" Annie asked, waiting for a response to her "Be careful" reminder.

"I definitely heard you, I'll definitely be careful, and now, please, definitely enjoy your soufflé and your birthday. Love you, Annie." I smiled, brown batter probably on my teeth but knowing Annie wouldn't mind one bit.

"Love you, too, Heids. Thanks for the necklace and for lunch." My best friend smiled back, and I was pleased to note chocolate smudged all over her central incisors.

◎ ◈ ◎

"Hurry up, you idiot!" I said aloud to the slow driver in front of me, immediately chastising myself for letting such unmotherly speech slip out in front of Nora. No mother wants her child to grow up to be the one calling her preschool teacher the "I" word when she takes too long lining up the kids for recess.

My belly happily digesting Sophie's soufflé, we headed home on Sycamore for Nora's nap and my precious two hours of freedom. "Freedom," of course, was a term I used loosely as it usually denoted wild parties involving laundry detergent, a mop, and, on raucous occasions, the toilet brush. Nevertheless, nap time was the closest thing I got to my time, so I guarded it ferociously.

I checked Nora in my rearview mirror and was alarmed to see her eyes drooping. Nora, unlike so many adaptable children, could not be transferred from car seat to crib without waking up. Instead, if she fell asleep on the way home to her real nap she would wake up in our driveway with bloodshot eyes and refuse to sleep again until nightfall. I stepped on the gas and flew through a traffic light of reddish hue.

"Norie," I sang, watching her eyes flutter open at my voice, "we're almost home, but you can't sleep . . . or from a building your mom may leap." Listen, I never claimed to be a poetry-writing Spanish teacher.

We turned off Sycamore and had about five minutes to go when my cell phone rang. Nora appeared grateful for the interruption to my dramatic recitation of the Pledge of Allegiance.

"Hello, this is Heidi."

"Heidi? Dr. Willard here."

"Hi, Dr. Willard. How are you?" I pictured him at his desk, wearing a short-sleeved gray dress shirt that did nothing for his figure, a widely knotted tie, and suit pants made of indestructible polyester.

"Fine, Heidi, fine. I'm calling with a small request, small request."

"What can I do for you?" I asked, trying to hear over Nora, who had conveniently begun to scream. At least she wasn't sleeping. The phone teetered on my shoulder while one hand rummaged blindly in my purse, the other hand gripping the steering wheel to prevent vehicular death. Jackpot. I found a tube of cherry ChapStick and morphed into Gumby to hand it back to Nora, who stopped wailing long enough to grip the shiny plastic.

"Well, it seems we have a bit of a challenge, see," Dr. Willard said. School administrators, like Amway salespeople, preferred "challenge" over "problem" or "catastrophe." We outsiders were not fooled.

"What's the problem?"

"Ahem, Ms. Stillwell is indisposed, effective immediately, and will be unable to finish the semester." He cleared his throat.

"Is she ill?" I asked, concerned. Had the kids finally pushed her over the edge? Had she crumpled under the pressure? Had the pip-squeaks triumphed?

"Yes, well, she'll really need to be the one who discloses that information," Dr. Willard said in a tone cryptic even by his standards. "I wonder, though, if you might be able to start a bit early and take over these last weeks before break. I know it's before you were planning on coming back, Heidi, but it'd really be in the students' best interests, their best interests."

I pulled into our driveway and turned off the ignition. Nora had tossed the lip balm into the back window. She looked dangerously relaxed in her seat. I bounded out of the car to rescue her from premature slumber and my certain doom.

"When would I start?" I asked, unhooking the sixty-five safety harnesses on Nora's car seat.

"We have a sub covering tomorrow, but I'd need you to start Monday."

Today was Thursday. That left three days before jumping back into the fray.

I turned my key and shoved open the front door with my free hip. Nora quit trying to prop up her head and rested it on my shoulder.

"I'll do it," I said. "I need to talk to my child care provider and to Jake, but plan on me coming on Monday unless you hear from me." My stomach flipped as I said the words.

"Marvelous, just marvelous," Dr. Willard gushed, his responsibilities neatly accomplished well before three o'clock, just the way he liked it. "See you Monday, then. And thank you, Heidi, thank you."

"You're welcome. See you soon," I said, snapping my phone shut while shedding my purse and Nora's diaper bag on the hallway floor.

I pulled Nora's blinds closed and held her to me while I lowered myself into her rocker. The darkened room acted as a stage cue; Nora closed her eyes immediately. She was out within seconds, her face and body completely relaxed and without a trace of her recent frantic plea.

I looked at her perfect face, astounded anew at the sheer beauty of someone sharing my humble genes. Her heart-shaped mouth parted slightly; her breath escaped in quiet rhythm. Her cheeks, rosy even in the dimly lit nursery, begged for me to kiss them, and I did gently, taking care not to wake her. She smelled like sky, like cotton sheets dried outside on the sunniest day. I closed my eyes, savoring the dark silence. Lowering Nora gently into the crib, I covered her with a soft blanket peppered with pink and green polka dots. She didn't move one centimeter.

A thought jarred me out of my silent admiration of my sleeping child. On Monday, this would be someone else's job. I felt my heart fill with something new, raw, breath-catching. My thoughts flew to a time the previous summer when I'd waved away and then slapped to Saturn a mosquito that had dared land on Nora's vulnerable neck. I'd trembled afterwards, clutched Nora to me, marveling at the ferocity of my love for her. Could anyone else love her like that?

I swallowed hard, touched my baby's forehead with my fingers, and tiptoed out of the nursery.

chapter/ten

Three loads of laundry, one and a half clean bathrooms, and two hours later, Nora woke from her nap. I heard her blowing spit bubbles into the baby monitor, and when I opened her door she kicked her arms and legs in greeting, smiling through a wayward pacifier she'd relocated and shoved in her mouth.

"Hello, peanut," I said, lifting her out of her crib and letting out a low whistle. "Whew, mama. Can you *smell* the poop?"

Mercy.

"No worries, dude. I'm all over it." I lowered her to the changing table, taking care to breathe through my mouth. Such a sweet child, yet capable of recreating Chernobyl in her diaper.

Clean pants in order, Nora ate her afternoon meal and was playing with a Tupperware bowl on the living room floor when I decided we should hop in the car and swing by Jake's work. I wanted to talk with him about Dr. Willard's phone call and knew he wouldn't be home until late because of the sale.

"Should we go see Daddy at work?" I asked Nora.

She seemed amenable, so I began The Gathering. It never ceased to amaze me how much gear was involved in transporting a child. I put some chewable toys into Nora's bag, along with extra diapers, wipes, and a complete change of clothes, knowing well the galactic possibilities involving fabric warfare. Step Two was to layer in a plastic bag of Cheerios, diaper rash cream, and a burping cloth. I trotted to Nora's room and collected her blankie, two pacifiers, and the fuzzy car seat cover. Finally, blueprints to Russian subs and underground shelters in the event of nuclear fallout.

Stuffing an increasingly mobile Nora into her winter coat caused me to break into a sweat, which, considering my need for aerobic exercise, made me feel efficient but dangerously out of breath. I coaxed Nora's dimpled hands through the cuffs, reminding myself to set up another gym date with Annie. Straightening up and hefting the loaded car seat into the crook of my arm, I lugged Nora, my purse, the diaper bag, and my sweaty self out to the car.

When I pulled up to Jake's store, I had to circle three times for a parking space. Elliott Paints was one of several paint stores in Springdale but the only one that was locally owned. Jake had not grown up here, but Springdale was small enough to care that his wife had. Elliott Paints' clientele was fiercely loyal, both to Jake and to the store's contribution to the local economy. Today was the end of the fall sale, and people were out in droves, cashing in on the last home improvement push of the year.

Nora searched above her for the bell that sounded as we pushed open the glass door. I could see Jake at the back helping a woman holding a blue and yellow lampshade. She was wrinkling her nose at the sixty-five paint swatches she'd already pulled; Jake was selecting a few more off the display.

I scanned the store and caught the eye of Jake's trusty side-kick. Rob Jeffries was busy ringing up sales behind the counter. He shot me a chin-up nod and waved me over.

"Hey, squirt," Rob said to Nora, smoothing her wind-blown coif. "You're getting bigger. Your mom and dad must feed you." He laid a beefy, paint-splattered finger on Nora's cheek and drew small circles. If she'd been a cat, she would have purred.

"Hi, Rob," I said, smiling up at him.

Rob was a big man. At six foot eleven, he had played basketball at Michigan State, helping the Spartans win the Big Ten Tourney and an NCAA title. He looked the part: sculpted arms, wide shoulders, stratospheric height. When we ground-lings cocked our heads in the right way, we could make out perfectly groomed sandy blond hair, kind eyes, and a white smile. Barbie's Ken on stilts and steroids.

"How are Samantha and the kids?" I asked.

Rob's wife stayed home with their four children — two girls, two boys. She was Rob's physical opposite, petite with dark hair and eyes. I often wondered if she kept a stepladder nearby for conversational purposes. Spousal communication had to get complicated when a girl struggled to be eye level with her husband's navel.

Rob finished ringing up a five-gallon drum for the customer at the counter. "Sam's fine, kids are fine. Joey broke his arm sledding last weekend, which almost made Coach Meyers pass out." Rob gave a goofy grin and rolled his eyes, having endured his share of neurotic coaches hungry for height under the basket. Joey, Rob's oldest, had inherited his father's frame and at twelve had already entered the world of adult fanaticism for children's sports. Fortunately, though, Samantha and Rob were far too stable to car bomb a referee or set the gymnasium on fire. Joey's broken arm was in good hands.

Rob and I chatted for a while between customers, and I was considering resorting to Ninja moves with Jake's lampshade lady when the two of them approached the register. Finally getting a chance to look up from Ivanna Trump, Jake's face lit up when he saw me and Nora. On cue, Nora produced a juicy spit-bubble greeting. Lampshade lady poured out a smile through ruby lipstick.

I waited to the side while Jake mixed and rang up a pint of Indigo Sky. All that for a lousy pint. A man of great patience, my husband.

When she'd left in her Lexus SUV, I hugged Jake and pecked him on the cheek. Nora gave her version of a hug, too, and Jake steered us toward his immaculate office in the back of the store.

I liked to think of myself as the creative one in our marriage, the one who was too busy worrying about self-expression and intellectual freedom to concern herself with mundane issues like dusting. I needed these self-assurances whenever I witnessed how Jake lived when I didn't encumber him.

Right in the middle of his most hectic week and Jake's desk was organized like a military general's. Colored bins daintily held neat stacks of mail and paper. A lone Post-it note was stuck on one side of his nameplate; a canister for paper clips flanked the other side. Otherwise, the desk was empty and spotless. My own desk at school was colorful, full of different textures, let's say. More Picasso, less Martha.

"To what do I owe this surprise?" Jake asked, taking Nora from me and setting her on his desk. He gave her a plastic paint stirrer for nibbling. One day the color wheel would entertain, but at this stage the danger of *eating* the wheel was still too great.

"I got a call from Dr. Willard," I said. "Stillwell's down for the count, circumstances unknown. Willard wants me back at school on Monday."

Jake raised his eyebrows at me. "What did you say?"

"I told him yes, but that I needed to talk with you and with child care. What do you think? Am I nuts to go back a month early?"

Jake was looking at his daughter, who had coated her purple winter coat with paint stick drool. "Can Rina take Nora early?" Rina was a German woman in her sixties who ran a day care out of her home. She'd come highly recommended by my colleagues at school, so I was thrilled when she'd agreed to take Nora when I returned to work in January. For the amount she charged, Rina was the one who should have been thrilled.

"I haven't called her yet, but I don't think it will be a problem."

Jake shrugged. "I think you should do what you want. Nora will miss you a month early, and I'm sure you'll miss her, but she'll adapt. And you'd feel better knowing you're not siccing another sub on your students, right?"

"Right," I nodded, a little disappointed Jake hadn't put up some sort of fight. If anyone could have encouraged me to wait out my entire leave, it would have been Jake. Maybe the sale hadn't been what he'd wanted and he was worried about our finances. Maybe he was secretly relieved I would return to work earlier, give extra padding to our bank account in time for Christmas.

Out of the corner of my eye, I could see someone standing in the doorway to Jake's office. Jake's face broke into a smile. I turned to see the recipient. A woman in a black turtleneck sweater, a chestnut ski vest trimmed with fur, and expertly tailored black pants stood in the threshold to the office. She had long straight hair the color of honey and round blue eyes.

"Beautiful" did not do this chick justice.

Though I suspected the effect was just as stunning without an ounce of makeup, her face had just enough eye shadow, blush, and lipstick to make you think she'd thrown it on at the last minute. Being a savvy female myself, I shrewdly suspected she'd taken roughly an hour prep time and spent half my monthly paycheck on the eyeliner alone. You can't get that look with Maybelline, let me assure you.

"Hey," the woman said, returning Jake's smile. Nora and I squinted at her perfectly straight and astoundingly white teeth, unaccustomed to such brightness. I could just imagine Annie checking out her veneers.

The woman made a motion to exit, a move that made me feel much more attractive. "I didn't know you had company; I'll come back. . . ."

"No, of course not," Jake said, jumping up from his chair. He gestured to the woman with an open hand and said, "Jana Van Fleet, this is my wife, Heidi, and our daughter, Nora."

Jana Van Fleet. We meet at last, and I hadn't seen a mirror since dawn. I stood and thrust forward my hand to distract her from my shiny forehead and unibrow. "It's nice to meet you, Jana," I said with a smile straight off one of Bob Barker's *The Price Is Right* girls. "I've heard so much about you."

Jana shook my hand, tossed her honey hair over her shoulder, a la Swedish ski bunny. "I hope only the good things," she said, looking at Jake and doing a Crest commercial. "Have you been nice?" she asked him, tipping her chin to one side.

"Of course," Jake said, still smiling. I found his glee completely obnoxious. "I'm an extremely nice person."

"Oh, I know that," said Jana, turning to me as Nora and I resumed our seat opposite Jake. "Jake has absolutely *saved* this project, which is saying a lot considering my bear of a father, not to mention my unreliable car." She looked at Jake with appreciation. "I owe him big-time."

I shuddered to think of all the ways in which Jana Van Fleet could settle a debt.

The air in Jake's office had been taken over completely by Jana's seven-billion-dollar perfume pressed from rare orchids on the thighs of virgin Amazon princesses. I breathed rapidly, trying to coax oxygen into my lungs.

Nora began to squawk, no doubt a side effect of gradual asphyxiation by orchids, and Jana looked her way for the first time. Her feline body moved from its station in the doorway, all one hundred five pounds of her in liquid motion. She leaned over Nora, and I was grateful she was wearing a turtleneck, as someone had done a magnificent job on her set of great, um, personalities.

"Oooh," she cooed, as only a woman with no children can. "Hello, there, little one. Nora, right?" Nora looked at her with wide eyes, no smile, for which I thanked her silently and promised to reward later with a Gerber biscuit. Jana purred, "You have your daddy's eyes, Nora, do you know that?"

I glanced at Jake, who was taking in the scene with great pride. Jana may as well have said Nora had just been named the youngest and smartest Supreme Court justice. I bolted suddenly from my chair, causing Jana to take a sudden step backward.

"We'll let you two talk business," I said, hefting Nora's bag over my shoulder and the baby onto my hip. Nora fussed, clawing for her lunch. As I was in my husband's office, I would normally have fed her right then and there. I looked at Jake, waiting to see if he'd catch on to the hierarchy of female needs.

Nope.

"Thanks for coming by, girls," said Jake, leaning over his desk to give Nora a kiss on the head and me a brotherly peck on the cheek. A quick image flashed through my mind of us wrapped into a deep, slobbery kiss on the desk, me peeking over Jake's shoulder as Jana Van Fleet crumpled to witness the force of such marital bliss and physical passion. I shook my head to clear it and smiled feebly at Jana.

"It was a pleasure to meet you," I said, totally comfortable lying through my teeth. Nora let out a wail that made Jana jump.

"My, my," she said, frowning in mock concern for my child's well-being. "Are we hungry? Is Mommy going to feed you?"

Yes, Mommy is, as a matter of fact. Mommy does a lot of things quite capably that you know nothing about, little Swede.

"We'll see you at home," I said to Jake, without a smile, though I tried, resulting in a smirk, also appropriate. "Have a good meeting." I arched my eyebrows at him and left through the doorway, now vacated. Jana had slinked over to my chair, still warm from the presence of a wife and innocent child. Home wrecker.

I nodded to Rob on my way out, glad he was busy with customers and wouldn't want to chat.

"Get a grip on yourself," I chided myself as I strapped Nora into her seat. "There is nothing going on between Jake and Jana Van Fleet. He loves *you*. He loves your daughter. He's just doing his job."

I pulled into traffic, identifying with the pathos of Nora's bitter weeping. I considered pulling off the road to nurse, but was too humiliated to think I'd be reduced to that after having to leave my own husband's private office. We pushed toward home, Nora screaming bloody murder and my heart pounding with adrenaline, like it had when I'd thrown up before every track meet in junior high.

Just what I want, I stewed. A marriage that makes me sick.

chapter/eleven

The first bell shrieked throughout Springdale High School, warning students that five minutes remained before pink tardy slips started to fly. Three tardies in the nine-week term meant after-school detention with Mr. Weinhöfen, the perpetually sweaty band teacher who slurped down pickled herring while students languished through their hour. Fishy aromas confined to a stuffy band room worked their magic: Springdale students had the fewest tardies in the state.

I made a last check of my lesson plans and took a swig of coffee. First day back and I felt pretty organized. I glanced at the framed photo of Jake and Nora on my desk and felt a sharp pang of guilt underneath the warmth of Colombian blend.

The drop-off at Rina's house had gone off without a hitch. Nora was befuddled by the early wake-up call, as I'd needed to be at school by 7:15, but she'd fixated on Rina's cocker spaniel, and my departure went unnoticed. Not sure if invisibility was good or bad, I'd wept like Tammy Faye Bakker all the way to work.

"Welcome back, Señora Elliott," Jessica Collins said, bounding into Spanish II in a flurry of blue and gold, Springdale's school colors. She wore a blue T-shirt with "SPIRIT" outlined in gold glitter, matching blue athletic pants and blue and gold running shoes. Her hair was in a high poof held up by an elastic band topped with mini blue and gold pompoms. All this pep and it was only eight o'clock on Monday morning.

"*Gracias*, Jessica." I smiled, leaning against my desk at the front of the room. "*¿Cómo estás hoy en día?*"

I saw panic flash across her face. "Are you going to break us in gently? To the Spanish, I mean. Seriously, like, Ms. Stillwell *never* spoke to us in Spanish."

Students flooded into the room, many of them wrecked after a weekend with too few hours for a teenager. Micah, sporting a vintage Twisted Sister T-shirt, nodded to me with eyes half-closed. Darren Smits slumped in his chair, head resting on his desk. Ana López gave me a wave while yawning. Austin Michaels was awake but ferociously scribbling in his honors chemistry lab book.

The second bell rang as Lindsay Patterson bolted through the door, all six feet of her. Lindsay would probably need to wait for college to find a boy who measured up to her, both in terms of height and maturity. She flew to her desk and slipped in with the grace of someone well acquainted with quick movement. "*Lo siento, Señora,*" she said when she saw me. "Sorry."

"*Está bien*, Lindsay," I said, moving to the middle of the room. I'd rearranged the desks over the weekend. Ms. Stillwell had preferred six straight rows, all facing the chalkboard, while I favored more of a community feel. This morning the desks were grouped in three semi-circles facing an open space in the middle of the room.

"Muy buenos días, chicos y chicas," I said, smiling at my compatriots. I'd missed them.

"Buenos días," they mumbled in return, some realizing for the first time that Ms. Stillwell had morphed into me.

Darren snapped his head up from its reclined position. His face broke into the grin that had nabbed him a spot on the homecoming court three years running. He did a fist pump and said, "Suh-weet! Stillwell bit the dust. You back for good, Mrs. Elliott?"

"Sí," Darren," I said, trying my best to feign disapproval but secretly happy to be higher on the list than Needlepoint Queen. "I've been warned this morning that your Spanish may be a little rusty."

Ana López snorted. While cute at sixteen, Ana had a face poised to be beautiful. Like everyone else in the room, though, she'd have to survive the perils of high school first. "Mrs. Elliott, you should go into diplomacy. Not only did Ms. Stillwell not know how to speak Spanish, she was afraid of us."

"I did feel bad when she'd cry," Lindsay said.

Ana raised her eyebrows at me. "See? So, yeah, we'll need a refresher course."

"Don't get too crazy on us, though," Darren said from the seat farthest back. He was wearing a rumpled Hawaiian shirt and threadbare jeans. "It's almost Christmas and plus, I'm swamped with college apps."

"Poor baby," said Ana with a roll of her eyes. I wondered if she had to exercise her eyeballs to be able to do that so fast. "Like the rest of us don't have lives, King Football."

"Listen, López," Darren started, looking the most awake he had this morning.

"All right," I interjected. "Enough. I get the hint. We'll take it easy for a few days until your mind relocates its Spanish-speaking lobe. But no dice on the Christmas thing, Smits," I warned. "Winter break is still three school weeks away, which is plenty of time to scare away your inner sloth."

"Great," Micah said, not looking up from a black notebook covered with hologram stickers. He nodded toward his class-mates. "They thought having a baby would mellow you out."

I grinned. "Okay. To begin, *o para empezar, hablemos de lo que hicieron El Día de Gracias.*"

I could almost hear the cogs grinding as the class looked at me blankly. After a while quiet Shanita Morrow risked, "What did we do for Thanksgiving? Is that what you want?"

"*Sí,*" I said, settling on the bar stool I kept at the front of the room. "Austin?"

Austin looked up from his lab notebook and shoved his glasses up the bridge of his nose. His nose was not, to quote a phrase, without spot or blemish. I wondered if I should keep him after class sometime and gently suggest a little Clearasil intervention. Austin would make ten times more money than any of the students I'd had over the years; his financial IQ put him in league with Warren Buffet. But this was still high school, and even future gazillionaires needed a date for Winter Formal.

Austin cleared his throat. "Um, *yo hizo,* um *hice,* I mean, *fui a la casa de mis abuelos.*" Went to Grandma's house. Perfectly rational and likely the truth. I couldn't see Austin going for a Thanksgiving ski romp to Vail.

"*Muy bien,* Austin," I said. "*¿Alguien más fue a la casa de los abuelos?*"

"I did, too," said Jessica. "However you say that in Spanish." She widened her eyes. "At least I knew what you were asking."

"*Mis abuelos viven en México*," Ana said, tapping her pencil on her desk. "They live in Veracruz and are appalled that their *nieta* doesn't speak *español* like a true *mexicana*." She was tapping the living daylights out of that pencil. "I'm pretty sure they'd be embarrassed to have me at their house for Thanksgiving, not that they celebrate Thanksgiving there."

Darren said from his slouch in the back, "You may not speak-o *el español*, but you do speak some dang good English, López, and you whip up in physics. Just tell 'em that." He was grinning at her from across the room. Ana, in an act of sheer brilliance, did not roll her eyes and instead smiled down at her dancing pencil, which slowed from the jitterbug to a fox trot.

Some other brave souls offered meek descriptions of their Thanksgiving experiences, and while none of them would be applying for UN interpreter anytime soon, I was encouraged to hear a few viable responses.

The other three periods before lunch were Spanish I, all of whom were still toiling onward with days of the week and months of the year. Nothing like prolonged lower-minded thinking to get one excited about a foreign language. We would wrap that up this week and move on to something a little more interesting, like knowing how to say, "My name is Jana Van Fleet and I steal husbands," or at least, "Where's the bathroom?"

Speaking of the Swedish princess, I made it all the way to third period before thinking of her and halfway through second before worrying about Nora's nap schedule at day care.

I felt smug with my professional, nonmommy behavior. In fact, I considered dropping in on Dr. Willard during passing period, sparkling through his office and making comments witty and carefree. But I had to use the time to call Rina and remind her to give Nora her blankie tag side up and to give her a tickle-rub on her back before sleep.

It was Day One for all of us, after all.

e ง e

Pork chops, beef for tacos, chicken breasts. I hurled various meat products into my cart as I flew through Tom's Ideal Grocery. Spending the weekend getting ready for school had meant bare cupboards, so I was at the store grabbing enough food to make it to Friday.

String cheese, eggs . . . did we need milk? My internal dialogue slipped outward every now and again, and I realized I was muttering the names of things I passed. A skinny brunette woman with two perfect children in coordinating polo shirts glanced at me, her smile pinched and worried about the woman before her who was either homeless and talking to invisible people or, gasp, a *working* mother too high-strung and stressed out to provide balanced meals for her neglected family. I bit my tongue to keep from sticking it out at her.

Halfway through the cereal and bread aisle, I took stock of my stuffed cart. It's true what they say about never going shopping around dinnertime. In haste and hunger, I'd grabbed six frozen pizzas, Oreos, three kinds of chips, Jimmy Dean sausage, and Popsicles.

1. I don't like frozen pizza.

2. Buying cookies and chips meant I would *eat* the cookies and chips, yielding unfortunate consequences.

3. I was a vegetarian in college and was morally opposed to the idea of sausage.

4. The last time I'd ingested a Popsicle was during the Reagan administration.

I sighed and added some Pop-Tarts to the mix.

Pushing toward checkout, via pancake mix and pasta sauce, I saw a familiar face. It was Willow, waving to me from her place in line. I waved back and steered my bulging cart behind hers.

"Hi," I said, genuinely happy to see a friendly face after a long day. "How are you?"

"Very well, thanks," Willow said, moving up a couple inches to allow more room for me and my cart. "Looks like you're on shopping duty tonight."

"This is my last stop before picking up Nora at day care, and I am ready to be home. The bummer is that I'll have to cook some of this before anybody eats, unless we become less afraid of salmonella."

Willow chuckled. "I vividly remember the harried dinner hour with small children. I developed a foul language problem between four and six every evening. Michael definitely did not approve."

I tried to imagine Willow cussing over her fry pan. She stacked her purchases on the conveyor belt: feta, sprouts, turkey bacon, grape tomatoes, organic milk. I was relieved to see a gallon of fudge tracks ice cream in the mix. A girl could get a complex.

"Are you back at work full-time, Heidi?" she asked, hands gripping an econo-size tub of yogurt.

"I am. It's earlier than I'd planned, but my substitute needed relief, so I'm back."

Willow searched my face. "How's the transition so far?" she asked.

"I'm doing okay," I said, surprised to feel a lump rising in my throat. "I really missed my work, so it's good to be back with my students. But I'm pretty tired." I stopped, then added, "And I miss Nora."

Willow nodded. "I remember feeling very conflicted, guilty no matter where I was. When I was at the gallery, I wanted to be with the kids. When I was with the kids, I wanted to hightail it to the gallery." She shook her head sadly. "I felt I couldn't win, which is a horrible way to feel twenty-four hours a day."

Willow took out her purse to pay as I began the task of unloading enough food for Nepal. When will I start winning again? I wanted to ask her. Tears blurred my eyes as I fumbled for the Cocoa Puffs. I refuse to cry in the checkout line, I thought angrily. I took a deep breath and kept unloading, not daring to look at Willow.

Between the pizzas and the Popsicles, I glanced over to the next row at a woman in high heels and an ankle-length mink. Not your usual grocery ensemble. But that perfect bod and those gargantuan breasts could mean only one woman: Jana Van Fleet.

Excellent. I love my life.

I ducked my head into my cart. Through the metallic grid I saw Jana plunk down a tin of mints. She pulled a gold card out of her Louis Vuitton and looked disoriented when he told her to swipe it. Apparently heiresses weren't accustomed to shopping with the serfs. She looked at her watch; I heard her say something about being late for the opera.

". . . Moms' Group this Wednesday." My ears rejoined Willow midsentence.

A boy with braces was loading Willow's bagged groceries into her cart. Willow buttoned up her coat and pulled down the ear flaps on her hat. She caught me staring at Jana and raised her eyebrows.

She waited, but I said nothing.

I couldn't possibly admit to Willow my insecurities about my husband's fidelity, particularly since Willow probably wished she had a husband to worry about at all. Besides, what could she say? That the Scandinavian goddess wasn't really *that* attractive? That I shouldn't worry about her being young and bendy? I stole another glance at Jana Van Fleet, standing feet away in all her PETA-insulting glory.

The odds were not in my favor.

"Yes," I gathered myself. "I'm planning on Moms' Group this week. I'll see you there." I paid the cashier and got my receipt. Willow walked with me toward the door. For once, I was thankful for the anonymity of being average; I would've had to run naked and screaming by Jana Van Fleet for her to notice me among all the other dowdy housewives in Tom's.

Willow and I pushed our carts in tandem through the sliding automatic doors. Soft snow blanketed the parking lot. A car passed in near silence, all sound muffled by the quilt of white. We stood for a moment, absorbing the quiet.

"You know, Heidi," Willow said. "We can't do everything. And we certainly can't do everything well. I wish I'd been more patient with myself over the years." She lifted her face to the falling snow. Tiny flakes landed on her freckled nose and cheeks, both beginning to blush in the cold air. "There's only one Savior of the world, and it's not me, even though I acted like I was for a long time." She looked back at me and smiled. "I hope I'll see you at Molly's. You take good care of yourself." She hugged me quickly before ducking her head and wrestling her cart through the snow to her car.

I unlocked my frozen door and kicked my snowy shoes against the floorboard before settling into the driver's seat. I clapped my mittens together, anxious for the heater to kick in.

I'll try taking better care of myself, Willow, I thought. But I've got a long way to go before mink and the opera.

chapter/twelve

The Langdon home cast warm light onto a snow-covered lawn. The moon's reflection on the white ground teased the night with unnatural brightness. My breath curled in wispy rivulets around my face while I waited for Molly to answer the doorbell.

After our third late dinner this week, I'd been relieved of dishes and Nora's bedtime regime by Jake, who was all too happy to get his tired and irritable wife out of the house for some QT with the Christians. I saw my attendance at Molly's house as repayment of a debt. Any group that would come to my aid when I couldn't breathe through either nostril deserved at least the courtesy of my participation in their little club. Not that I planned on saying or doing anything. In fact, I'd be happiest if Molly would just offer me one of those cushy chairs, hand me an afghan, and wake me up when it was all over.

"Heidi! Come in out of the cold, you poor thing," Molly said in a lowered voice. She was wearing a yellow and pink checked blazer with Star Trek–size shoulder pads. "We've just begun our discussion, but feel free to get refreshments in the kitchen and then join us when you're ready." She hugged me around my parka. What was it with these people? Did Jesus hug or something?

Molly returned to the group, and I hung up my coat on a burgeoning rack in the front hall. The entryway lighting was subdued, the staircase paintings lit by dimmed halogens mounted above their frames. I spotted Willow's llama coat and was glad she was here. Stepping gingerly around the lethal water feature, I headed to the kitchen.

Someone had brought a triple chocolate and peanut butter cheesecake and had perched a card in front to label it. I lobbed off a generous serving, feeling my taste buds tingle. Maybe tonight's discussion centered around the seven deadly sins and I could serve as visual aid for "gluttony."

I filled a mug with hot tea, balanced my loaded plate with a fork and napkin, and headed quietly into the great room.

"So if Peter tells us to focus more on our inner self than our outward appearance," Molly was asking the group, "how does this look on a day-to-day basis?"

Numbers were down a bit from the first time; ten or so women were gathered in the huge room, made cozy by a roaring fire stoked with cedar logs. I surveyed the congregants, looking for an unoccupied seat, preferably in a corner. I recognized the big blonde woman with a name tag that read "Shelly!" I smiled at Willow, who caught my eye from across the room, and took my seat next to Neesha, who patted my arm as I joined her on a love seat near the back.

"For one thing," said Laura Ingalls Wilder from a big chair that swallowed her and her slacks whole, "I think it means we should reorder our priorities of time and money. If we're spending more time or money on our physical appearance than on the things of God, we need to rethink our focus." She looked at Molly with a hopeful face, and I wished for her sake that Molly would cough up a nice big star to slap on Laura's Bible.

"Whew. More money for God than for us," Molly said, shaking her head of big hair. "That's tough. Much easier said than done."

I'd missed a few weeks, but I wondered how everything had gone with the pierced Ingalls daughter. Apparently the "physical appearance and personal finances" lesson had not yet passed from mother to daughter, as a few pairs of slacks couldn't possibly add up to one quality belly ring.

I shoved a big bite of cheesecake into my mouth.

"I know I don't follow that rule," said a new one sitting on the floor near the hearth. Her tag said "Sadie," and I had a feeling she and Laura shopped at very different stores. Sadie was an attractive woman with straight brown hair past her shoulders and round brown eyes. Her skin glowed with such brilliance, she was either (a) nine years old, or (b) getting surgical help. Her clothes spanked of those stores that carry only one of each item, arranged around an heirloom orchid or above a square of sod.

"I love clothes, I love shopping, and I love to look nice," Sadie confessed, looking at us in turn. Her ramrod posture spoke of many hours with a personal trainer. "I don't know if I can look like a slob in the name of Jesus."

Molly laughed. "Well, Sadie, I hope you won't. The Bible says nothing about being a slob. In fact, there are plenty of references to women and men adorning themselves, taking care

of themselves to honor a God who *created* physical beauty."
Molly stopped, tipped her chin upward in thought. "Perhaps
the point is whether our outward appearance is more important to us than the condition of our heart."

Neesha nodded and said, "I want my daughters to know
that order of business. Heart first, face and body a distant
second."

"What in the world are all you skinny wenches even
complaining about?" Shelly! roared from her seat on a couch,
startling Laura to the point of spilling her tea onto a red suede
ottoman. "Try thinking heart first when you can barely fit
into a movie seat." She shook her head, eyes sparking. "It's
hard to be nice to skinny people sometimes," Shelly! muttered.
"Bunch of whiners."

I scooped out an enormous bite of cheesecake, perhaps in
big girl solidarity, and waited for someone to respond. Shelly!
had fire, and I hoped someone would start it up with her, just
to sample some church lady theatrics.

Molly looked cool as a shoulder-enhanced cucumber in
her chair by the fireplace. For reminding me so vividly of
Kathie Lee Gifford in polka dots, Molly was really stepping up
when it came to this group. This woman was not intimidated
by violent outbursts or their ensuing silences.

Finally, Sadie, with the courage of a mouse, said, "I
certainly didn't mean to offend you, Shelly. I just wanted to be
honest for once, with myself, about who I am, what I like to
do." She shrugged, looking a little forlorn. "It didn't occur to
me to be a weight issue."

Shelly! blurted, "Exactly! That's what I am saying. Unless
it's *your* issue, weight is *not* an issue." She scanned the room,

perhaps looking for her next sparring partner. I thought of offering to get someone another slice of cheesecake, as it was *amazing*, but judged the gesture ill-timed.

Silence again. And then I think the peanut butter got to my head because from my formerly safe and inconspicuous perch in the back, guarded effectively by the calm and noncombative Neesha, I spoke. "Shouldn't we keep in mind that this Peter guy was a man? I mean, doesn't that count for something?"

Molly, perhaps surprised her young recruit would choose this as a safe entrance into the Moms' Group dialogue, raised her neatly waxed brows at me and said, "How do you mean, Heidi?"

It's not too late to go back, said my head while my tired mouth forged triumphantly onward. "I just think that for a man to write two thousand years ago that I should get my priorities in order is a bit presumptuous. I mean, who *was* this guy? I can't imagine he had an inkling into what my life would be in the twenty-first century." I forked another bite of cheesecake, waiting for the uproar of support from my female compatriots.

Not exactly, but I did see a few nods here and there.

A woman I didn't recognize but whose tag said "Andrea" asked, "Wasn't he the one who talks later about submission?" She shuddered.

Pockets of conversation sprouted up around the room. I wasn't sure what I'd started, but that reference to submission appeared to be riling these girls up. In a less exhausted state, I might have been more cautious, but as it stood I was happy to be entertained by the buzz of Christian bumblebees. Nothing short of a cheesecake-eatin' Virginia Woolf, I was.

Willow cleared her throat and said over the din, "As far as your question of who Peter was, Heidi, he was one of the twelve disciples. He was in the inner circle, one of Jesus' closest friends. But he betrayed Jesus three times in a row after Christ was arrested to be crucified." Her big eyes shone with wonder. The light from the fire sparked reflection off her hoop earrings. "Peter fell from the heights to inhabit with the bottom feeders. He denied ever knowing the Man who gave him new life, and yet Jesus restored him to their friendship and made him the rock on which the church was built."

She paused. The room drank in her silence, waiting.

"So Peter knew firsthand the value of a clean heart, free of all the dirt and grime. Maybe that makes him more credible." Willow took a sip of her tea, watching me.

Frankly, I wasn't really up to duking it out about the rock of the church. I'd only wanted to stir things up a little, maybe make some of the wheels in here turn in a different direction. Weary, I shrugged and said, "I just want to make sure we're being fair about this. I mean, when someone in a couple millennia reads my journals, I'll be perfectly fine with them considering the source. No offense."

Willow smiled into her tea, and Molly quickly said, "And no offense taken, Heidi. I think you've raised some very important points concerning the cultural relevance of Scripture. This is an enormous subject, and I think we should revisit it again. For now though," and she sighed, probably with relief, "we need to close in prayer. Any requests?"

We made our way through petitions for a new job, patience with an unruly toddler, and what I think was a request for a new husband. I listened to each woman who asked for prayer, and I thought I just might try. Couldn't hurt, I figured, though that may very well have been the cheesecake talking. I felt my body sink into the love seat cushions as Molly prayed, fighting sleep within an inch of my life.

A chorus of "amen" startled me out of half sleep, and I opened my eyes too wide as compensation. I hefted my body off the love seat and said good-night to Neesha, who patted me on the arm again and said into my ear, "Girl, you need to go home and sleep. I *know* you didn't make it all the way through that prayer." She winked and walked away.

At least I hadn't drooled.

I was outside on the front sidewalk when Molly called after me. She scooted out carefully to where I was. She walked with arms extended like a tightrope walker, coatless and shivering. I gasped when she came close to cashing out on the frozen walkway.

"Heidi," she said when she reached me, "I hope you know we love having you here." Her teeth chattered; she clung to my arm to keep from falling. "I want you to feel completely at home and able to say what's on your mind." She added, "You picked an interesting topic with which to introduce your thoughts to the group, but I hope you felt at ease." Coming from my piano teacher in elementary school, this would have been lightly veiled criticism, but coming from Magenta Molly, I knew she meant it.

"Thanks, Molly. You're nicer even than Jake thought, and he thinks you're the sweetest woman on earth." Blue lips smiled at my compliment. I put my arm around her and guided her gently toward her front door. "Now get back inside before I inadvertently kill the group leader with hypothermia. I'm pretty sure there's some serious 'Don't murder' talk in that Bible of yours."

Molly gave a little frozen giggle and scurried back inside. I turned and headed back to my car, to my home, to my bed. My ignition turned over right away, despite the frigid temperatures. I yawned a Thank You that I'd made it to December without having to use jumper cables.

Pulling around Magnolia Circle, I tried reviewing what had just happened. Really, I did. My eyes were droopy, though, and the synapses weren't as spry as they used to be. I decided I'd have to think about Peter, submission, and cultural relevance tomorrow. This twenty-first century girl needed her beauty rest.

chapter/thirteen

"You look really good, babe," I said, tucking my legs into the car and shutting the passenger side door. I leaned over and kissed Jake's cheek. "I feel such pity for the women who didn't marry you, which makes me a lady of many sorrows." I warbled a few bars of "We Are the Champions," gloating over my mating good fortune.

"You're awfully chipper this evening," Jake said flatly. His eyes were on the road, but his right hand fiddled with the radio and the thermostat, neither yet to his liking.

"I *am* chipper, in fact, and have many reasons to be. Shall I enumerate them for you?" Not waiting for an answer, I ticked off points on my newly painted fingernails, fire engine red, thank you very much. "First," I began, "I'm wearing a dress that is neither utilitarian nor in the least bit teachery. Not that I'm usually seen in wooden apple necklaces or calico jumpers, God bless my colleagues, but I'm feeling rather smug to be in a little black number instead of work clothes or mom wear." I looked down for emphasis, pleased with myself. Annie's Gestapo techniques had finally kicked in. She was thrilled with her chart and I with the definition in my calves.

"Second, a point closely connected to my first, seven months after birthing, I finally fit into said little black number. This is a feat to be ranked right up there with *glasnost* and getting O.J. an acquittal."

Jake at last seemed happy with the temp and the tunes, but said nothing in response to my crowing.

"Third, I'm out to dinner with my husband and without my daughter, whom I love but am happy to relinquish to Super Lauren for the evening. And last," I summed up, "I am hungry and going to be fed at my all-time favorite restaurant, Maurizio's Italian Bistro. In short, I'd like to thank all the little people who got me to this point and my parents for always believing in me."

I pulled my compact from a sassy beaded pocketbook I'd used three times in my entire life. A check in the little mirror, quick touch-up with the lipstick. . . . It was official: I was still a girl.

Jake pulled into Maurizio's small parking lot and found an empty spot. We were out early; the place was nearly empty. For twenty years, Maurizio Chiaramonte had quietly run the best restaurant in town. His place was housed in the cellar floor of a brick building covered with ivy. That his remarkable cooking also happened to be Italian was just an extra bonus for me. Somewhere, somehow, my genealogy must have included Mediterranean roots that caused me to crave handmade pasta and bruschetta drowned in ripe tomatoes and fresh basil. Maurizio's gave me my fix on this side of the Atlantic, smack-dab in the middle of the heartland.

Jake held open the door for me, and I strode into Maurizio's small and intimate dining room. The decor was understated.

Plain white tablecloths were set with small vases of dahlias. Two of the walls retained their original function and were filled with wine bottles from floor to ceiling. The brick floor was worn and uneven in places, underscoring the clandestine feel of the place. While the Chiaramontes were not in the running for any awards in interior design, they focused on food and service, both of which had kept loyalists like Jake and me coming back lasagna after lasagna.

As we waited to be greeted in the tiny candlelit foyer, intoxicated by the smell of Maurizio's menu, I absorbed the prolonged silence on Jake's end. "Everything okay?" I ventured. "You seem kind of quiet."

Jake waited a few moments and said, "I'm okay. Just a little confused."

I quizzed him with my eyebrows as the host checked our reservation and showed us to our table. Our waiter arrived to recite the specials, several of which made my salivary glands go into overdrive. I'd wondered at times if I was overly impressed with food. I'd probably be a much more well-rounded person if I got that excited about, say, art history or bocce ball.

I closed my menu and watched the host, Silvio, who was a cousin or maybe nephew of Maurizio, scurry around like a squirrel before winter. Jake and I were virtually alone in the dining room. One college couple canoodled in a corner, and a man sat alone near the host's stand, reading a book and lingering over his after-dinner cappuccino.

After our waiter had delivered our beverages, I returned to the question at hand. "What confuses you?"

Jake perused his menu with a furrowed brow. His eyes passed methodically over the selections, and I had to bite my cheek to keep from laughing. Why bother, I wondered, when you know exactly what you're going to order? I was willing to place a heavy wager, say, the sale of our house and both cars, on chicken ravioli with wild mushrooms. My husband mixed paint all day. He liked formulas, predictability, order, and schedules. He'd ordered the ravioli every single time we'd eaten at Maurizio's since college. I'd eat my shorts if he wavered tonight.

Jake cleared his throat. "I'm confused about why it's so hard for you to be honest with me about Ben."

Holy moly. Where was this coming from?

"He stopped in the store today," Jake continued, reaching for a piece of bread, dipping it in olive oil. I waited as he chewed. "He's painting some rooms in his house, and he was a total pain in the neck until he got one particular neutral for the living room. He said this was a double whammy, as his living room would also be his work space."

Oh, dear.

Jake looked up. "He's shooting there this weekend, he said. A piece about American women for his fancy schmantz New York editor. Hadn't Heidi told me, he asked? About the shoot? About Heidi and Nora's special feature within the assignment?"

"Jake," I said in a measured tone, "hold on a minute. First of all, I have meant to tell you about this many times, but for one reason or the other, it has slipped my mind."

Jake snickered, a noise unbecoming to a man of his age.

"I'm serious," I said. "Plus, it's no big deal. Such a nondeal, in fact, that I haven't thought about it since he asked me to do it." Not much, anyway. And certainly not when on my first date in months. Good grief, did we have to talk about this now? I remained calm, hoping my nonchalance would inspire confidence in Jake and that he'd drop it so I could enjoy my black dress and manicotti.

"That's exactly why I'm confused, Heidi," Jake said with emphasis. "I think it *is* a big deal and that's precisely why you never mentioned it. I don't think you wanted me to know."

"Wait just a minute, bud," I said, starting to lose my cool. Our waiter interrupted us and asked if we needed more time to decide. I ordered first, then sat back to sip my wine while Jake ordered.

"I'll have the Gorgonzola gnocchi, please. And a garden salad to start." He snapped shut his menu and I balked. Okay, perhaps many people wouldn't see a change in pasta affinities as a marital watershed, but this was Jake Elliott. Good old Andy Griffith–lovin' Jake and Gorgonzola gnocchi? I didn't even know he knew how to pronounce it.

"Gnocchi?" I asked as the waiter left. "You never told me you liked gnocchi."

"You never asked," Jake said, shrugging. "Besides, if I had to rank them, I would think secret meetings with ex-boyfriends would edge out secret fondness for pasta on a scale of importance." Jake dipped another piece of bread and chomped down on a huge bite.

"Secret meetings, huh?" I could feel my willpower tumbling downward into the "no self-control" zone. "If we're going to go down that road, why don't we just open all the hatches and talk about rainstorm rendezvous with a certain heiress?"

Jake scrunched up his face into a question mark and then the lightbulb. "You mean Jana? Heidi, you cannot be serious. I was helping her with a faulty ignition."

"I'm *sure* you were," I practically sneered. I looked past Jake, took a sip of wine. "Listen," I said. "Did it ever occur to you that I might not have said anything because I knew, deep in my honest subconscious, that you would freak out like this and misunderstand the entire situation?"

Jake returned my hard gaze tit for tat. "You lived with him. You slept with him. You've known him your whole life, and he's vacationed with your family. I think I have reason to feel uncomfortable."

I closed my eyes, took a long, slow breath, opened my eyes, and looked into Jake's. "All of those things are true and absolutely out of my control to change. But can't you trust me, Jake? I'm married to you. I chose *you*."

He looked down at his hands. He unfolded them and began brushing breadcrumbs into a neat pile. "Fine," he said with resignation. "I trust you."

"Fine," I echoed.

We ate our salads in silence. Our waiter cleared the dirty plates, exchanging them for our pastas. Manicotti and gnocchi absorbed all the attention at our table. Neither of us ventured a glance upward but kept our eyes securely on southern Italy. Not really the way I'd envisioned the evening, negotiating a precarious truce. If I'd been more energetic, I would have tried to figure out when being careful of each other had become so important, when caution had trumped transparency. But the last week had left me depleted. Work, Nora, and Jake engaged in hot competition for only one me, and I was beat.

So I shut up and ate.

This arrangement allowed for ample people-watching time. At one table hugging the back wall, a man and woman sat hunched over the white tablecloth, intent in conversation. I could barely make them out in the dim lighting, but as I looked longer and tried to squint without blowing my cover, I could see the woman's shoulders trembling slightly, arms gathered tightly to her sides. She wiped her eyes and blew her nose occasionally. I wasn't sure I would have taken much notice had it not been for the nose blowing, which I recognized immediately.

"Ms. Stillwell?" I asked in a disbelieving whisper. Did Stillwell have a boyfriend? And wasn't she supposed to be ill? My first week back at school had been so hectic, I hadn't made time to call and ask about her health. I'd made a mental note to ask Rachel Davis if she knew why Ms. Stillwell had left in such a rush, but in the flurry of day-to-day, I hadn't gotten around to my inquiry.

"Who?" Jake asked. He polished off the remaining gnocchi and grabbed the last slice of bread to mop up the sauce.

"Ms. Stillwell," I whispered back, jerking my head in her direction. "I'm pretty sure that's my substitute teacher who had to leave under shady circumstances. I think she's crying."

Jake, not known for his subtlety, whipped his head right, then left, then a full one-eighty to hunt for a crying Stillwell.

"Could you be a bit more discreet?" I hissed, busying myself with the napkin in my lap. "James Bond, not Barney Fife."

"Who's she with?" Jake asked, finishing off his meal with a gulp of wine. His eyes still did not meet mine, but he was talking. Baby steps.

"I'm not sure," I said, peering around Jake to catch a glimpse of the man with Stillwell. My view of him was obstructed almost entirely by Stillwell's back, but I could see he had reached across the table to take her hands. He looked to be only slightly taller than Stillwell, maybe big around the middle. His shoulders were tense, and he leaned forward in his chair until his face was only inches from hers. Whatever these two were discussing, I wished for a closer seat to eavesdrop. Jake hadn't talked to me with that intensity since the Lewinsky scandal. He was a straight-ticket Republican, so I'll bet you can guess what the intensity was all about.

All the way through tiramisu and cappuccino, I watched Stillwell's table out of the corner of my eye. The couple was so engaged in hushed, impassioned conversation that she never once looked in my direction. We were waiting for the check and I'd begun to think I'd never know the identity of Mystery Man when they rose from the table. Still with his back to me, Mystery helped Stillwell with her coat, stopping to plant one on her tear-streaked lips. I ducked behind my dessert menu as they moved toward the foyer to leave. When they were nearly to the door, I saw his face and gasped.

"You've *got* to be kidding me," I whispered, still behind the dessert menu.

"What's going on?" Jake asked. He completed a meticulous signature on the credit card receipt and moved back to examine his work. I knew he was calculating the tip again to make sure he'd given exactly fifteen percent. Having endured years of waiting tables in order to pay for school, I enjoyed tipping like Trump. My husband, who detasseled corn each summer, thought rounding up was for sissies.

Satisfied, he tucked the yellow copy into his billfold.

I was reeling. "Jake, Stillwell just left with Dr. Willard."

"Is that weird?" Jake asked, pushing back his chair to go.

"Well, it wouldn't be if Dr. Willard weren't married to Mary Jo Willard. And it gets a whole lot weirder considering I saw him *kiss* Ms. Stillwell." My thoughts spun like windmills. Does this mean Willard is having an *affair* with Stillwell? Isn't that illegal? Is that why she left the sub job prematurely? Will I have to go into therapy after seeing Dr. Willard kiss a woman?

"Not good," Jake said, the irony of the situation and our dinner conversation not lost on either of us. "Let's go," he said, waiting for me to button my coat.

We thanked Silvio and asked him to pay our compliments to the chef, then pushed open the door to the blue-black of the winter twilight. Jake hurried a few paces ahead to start thawing the car. The passenger side door creaked as I opened it. I sat shivering under my seatbelt, watching Jake scrape the windshield in even, efficient strokes. The frozen dust gathered at the perimeter, then flew off the car with a sweep of Jake's brush.

On our way home, I watched the streets pass outside my cleared window, thinking of Stillwell, Jake, Ben. I pictured Nora all warm and snuggly in her crib, peacefully oblivious to the fact that her parents had personalities, dreams, and arguments. I glanced at Jake, his face illuminated by the glow of the dash lights, and wondered how long we'd be able to fool her.

ℰ ℈ ℰ

The next morning I woke before Jake and Nora, which put me on par with elderly people and Matt Lauer. An elusive

Saturday morning sleep-in stung after such a tiring week. I lay beside Jake, forcing my eyes closed, wishing I had one of those white noise machines from Sharper Image. I'd have gone for the "babbling brook" setting. Maybe "roaring fire."

After trying for twenty minutes to convince my body to keep sleeping, I succumbed to wakefulness and slipped out of bed.

Burrowing my feet into fuzzy purple slippers, I wrapped my thick fleece robe tightly around my body, convinced I could see my breath clinging to the air in front of me. I snuck out of our bedroom and took a spin by the thermostat to raise it to a temperature habitable by humans. Jake, the fifteen percent tipper, was also the heat and air-conditioning Nazi. Woe to the woman who innocently raised or lowered the thermostat without written permission from Keeper of the Bills. I hiked the temp five full degrees and smiled smugly into frosty air. There were advantages of being early to rise.

In an uncharacteristic burst of morning energy, I decided to play homemaker and make a breakfast that went beyond tossing flakes into a bowl or plugging in the toaster. Waffles, scrambled eggs, bacon, and orange juice, I decided, starting up the coffeemaker with resolve. Little tinges of guilt tried to rain on my altruistic gesture. If honest with myself, perhaps I would have to admit I was trying to make up for my shoddy spousal communication and, even more so, my absentee mothering of the last week. I quietly went about my business, mixing up waffle batter, stirring up orange juice, and cracking eggs.

It had been a while since I'd done Betty Crocker. I had to do a backbend that Mary Lou Retton would have envied in order to drag the waffle iron out of the bowels of my pantry, and it was nothing short of miraculous that we even had bacon in the house. But I soldiered on, feeling proud to provide a hearty breakfast for my small brood.

"Morning," Jake said in his I'm-barely-awake voice. He rubbed his eyes, and I saw how he must have looked when he was seven years old and up for Saturday morning cartoons.

"Morning, hon," I said, hoping last night's discussion hadn't carried over into a new day. I poured out a waffle and shut the iron, taking a deep breath through my nose in anticipation.

Jake poured himself a cup of coffee and leaned against the counter, watching me. "What's all this about?"

"Just wanted to make some breakfast for the Elliott family," I said. I laid strips of bacon into the hot skillet and smelled the immediate gratification of this little piggy going to market. My coffee was working its magic, I knew, as I started to feel energized by cooking at such an ungodly hour.

Jake watched me in silence, sipping his coffee and letting it slowly awaken his rumpled face. The waffle iron light went on, and I turned out the first golden brown lovely of the morning. Dropping it onto a plate, I added bacon and scrambled eggs and handed the feast to Jake.

"Can I get you some toast or orange juice?" I asked, getting the syrup and butter out of the fridge.

"I'm good, thanks," he said, putting the plate on the counter and picking up a slice of bacon to munch. "Heidi, about last night . . ."

I shut the door of the refrigerator and turned to look at him. "Yes?" I thought I'd leave the ball in his court at this point. I *was* making the Iron Family breakfast, after all. Didn't Aunt Jemima count for something?

"I think it's okay that you do that photo shoot with Ben," Jake said, his eyes tired. The coffee must not have reached that high yet. "I can't say I'll sing his praises or ever really like him, but I trust you to behave yourself."

I winced at the word "behave." What did he think this was? A field trip in second grade and I needed a permission slip?

"Jake," I began, turning the second round of bacon. I had no chance for rebuttal, however, because Nora woke up crying her head off. From the monitor, it sounded like she was being eaten by wolves, but the astute and experienced mother in me knew not to panic: merely a hungry baby in search of a nipple.

Jake stopped chewing and stared at the monitor, looking worried. It had been a while since he'd witnessed the "Hey slackers, I'm *starving* in here" yelp of early morning. Not quite the Superman welcome he returned to after work.

"Is she all right?" he asked, eyes big. "Should I go get her?"

"She's fine, just hungry," I said, already on my way to the nursery. "You can't help her very much at this point." There are times when being the life sustainer of your child is rewarding, when the knowledge that you are feeding her exactly what she needs makes you feel like belting out "The Circle of Life." And then there are times when breastfeeding is a big, lactating pain in a lumpy, postpartum rear.

Waffles, bacon, and Dr. Phil conversation with the husband would have to wait.

ℰ ℈ ℮

Twenty minutes later, I emerged with Nora. She gurgled happily on my hip, oblivious to the wrongness of appearing before the sun. Jake's syrup-coated plate rested in the sink; I could hear the clunk of our shower head kicking in.

With Nora deposited in her high chair, I began cutting up a leftover waffle into baby-appropriate pieces, big enough to grasp, small enough to slide. I went easy on the syrup and took Nora's breakfast, Part *Deux*, to the table.

"This is a waffle," I said, holding up a little square. "Want to try it?"

A silly question, as Nora had never excelled at self-denial, particularly when it came to putting foreign objects in her mouth. She gripped the waffle and gummed it for a while. Judging from the wild-eyed slurping and sucking noises, Nora liked syrup. In fact, it looked like she'd prefer to forego the waffle altogether and open her mouth under a maple tap in the New Hampshire woods.

"Morning, sweetie," Jake said, leaning to kiss her sticky cheek. "Are you having your first waffle experience?"

Nora kept sucking the juice out of the waffle square, barely lifting her eyes to acknowledge Jake. There comes a time in every girl's life when Daddy can't compete with a first love.

Even amid lingering bacon aromas, I could detect the clean and showered smell of Jake-in-the-morning. "Are you leaving?" I asked.

"Yeah, I'm afraid so," he said, though he didn't look so sorrowful to me. "I have to head to a couple of sites this morning to check on progress."

I thought about asking if one of said sites was the Van Fleet job, but I cringed at lowering myself to the meddling wife. Instead, I asked, "Will you be home at all today? Maybe we can take Nora to the children's museum or go watch ice skaters in the park?"

"I'll have to see," Jake said, busy wrapping himself in a scarf. It was a beautiful shade of indigo, an exact match to his eyes. From where I sat with Nora, the scarf looked an awful lot like cashmere, not the typical choice for a man who skimps on heating costs.

"Nice scarf," I admired. "Where'd you find it?"

Jake pulled on black leather gloves and took his wool coat off its hanger. "Gift from a client," he said into the closet.

I felt a lump rising in my throat. Gift from a client. Someone who could afford cashmere as a token of appreciation to her painter? I jumped up from the table to move back into the kitchen, squeezing in hot tears that threatened to fall. Don't ask, I commanded myself. You don't really want to know the answer to that question.

I inhaled shakily, blinking madly as I pretended to look for something in the fridge. I grabbed the pitcher of orange juice, which I tipped into my coffee mug. Drops of brown diluted into orange swirls.

Jake's kiss on my cheek made me jump.

"I'll call you," he said, walking toward the door after another stop at Nora's cheek.

"Okay," I called, still staring into my cup. "Have a good morning."

Jake shut the door behind him but not before a gush of freezing air trampled over the threshold. I shivered back to Nora, who frantically scanned the room for any sign of Mrs. Butterworth.

"Here, peanut," I said, putting a few more waffle squares on her tray. She kicked her drumstick legs in gratitude.

"What do you think, peanut?" I asked, sipping my muddy cocktail. "What should we do this morning?" She watched me, her mouth outlined in sticky crumbs. "How about a walk in the mall?"

Silence.

"Yeah, I don't really feel like braving the pre-Christmas crowds, either. Hmm . . . what about a visit to Aunt Annie? It's the weekend, so she has the day off."

"Sheoimrosh," Nora said around a sticky hand wedged in her mouth.

"I'll give her a call," I agreed, walking toward the cordless phone in the kitchen. Before I could hit speed dial, the phone let out a shrill ring, nearly causing me to jump out of my robe.

"I was just about to call you," I answered, sure only Annie would call this early on a Saturday morning. I pictured her in winter running gear, stretching on her hardwood floors after an early seven miles. Love her, love her compulsions.

"You were?" asked an amused male on the other end. "I'm glad to be on your mind this early in your day."

Ben. Holy cow. How did I look?

"Hi, Ben. How are you at this hour?" I wet a paper towel and brought it to Nora, whose face resembled a painting by Dalí.

"I'm great, ready for a good day's work," Ben replied. "In fact, I was hoping you and Nora could join me. I'm sorry it's such late notice, but I'm running ahead of schedule and was hoping you'd be free this morning."

I halted Nora's ascent midair as I lifted her out of her chair. I made a quick mental checklist of the facts: Jake had left us to entertain ourselves on a weekend morning while he gallivanted around in a cashmere scarf, likely with the scarf giver herself. I was being asked to spend the morning with my ex-boyfriend. But the reasons were entirely professional, and my child would be there, for goodness' sake. Plus, Jake had magnanimously given his permission, whatever that meant.

"As a matter of fact, I'm wide open," I said, decided. "Nora and I were just discussing what we'd do today and hadn't come up with anything." Sorry, Annie.

"Perfect. How soon can you be here?"

I looked at my reflection in the microwave door. "We'll see you in forty-five," I said, already untying my robe on the way to the shower. Nora giggled at the wild ride she was getting on my hip.

"Thanks so much, Heidi. I'll see you soon," Ben said, and the phone clicked.

"No, thank *you*, Ben," I said aloud, pushing the button to hang up. "You've given me the perfect diversion to what began as another cold and frosty morning."

chapter/fourteen

A wise woman once told me temptation is easy to avoid — you just have to be dead. I was alive and kicking that Saturday morning, which helps to explain how my head and heart collided in a downward spiral.

We walked the short distance to Ben's house. Nora rode in her SUV stroller, while I pushed her along the sidewalks. Our outdoor thermometer read thirty degrees, but there was no ice on the walkways and I was desperate to clear my lungs and my mind with a little fresh air. Nora chattered gaily beneath her multiple layers of clothing and blankets. I checked her periodically to make sure she hadn't lost any appendages to frostbite. My mother's voice echoed in my head, accusing me of allowing Nora to "catch her death," but I walked briskly and hummed above her preaching. Surely even she, if pressed, would have remembered the rabid panic to get outdoors after being cooped up with an infant for months of Midwestern cold.

"You okay in there, peanut?" I asked, taking the corner of Ben's street at a clip.

"Eeeee!" Nora yelled with gusto. Sounded good to me.

Three houses before Ben's, I nodded to a man putting up his outdoor Christmas lights. No blinkers or chasers in this neighborhood—Ben lived in straight-up white light territory. The artsy few were forgiven their preference for big multicolored bulbs, their neighbors chalking it up to vintage chic. But refrain, please, from the fake icicles so popular these days. If you liked those, you were better off in the suburbs.

Seventeen Hollowbrook Road emitted a soft glow into the tentative light of morning. Ben's home was cozy, extending to stroller pushers the promise of warmth. A bungalow built in the thirties, the house could have leaped off the pages of the Pottery Barn catalog, complete with wide covered porch and Arts and Crafts light fixtures. The wood siding had been painted recently in a moss green with crisp ivory trim. The floor of the front porch was a weathered red. Well-used and much-loved porch chairs and a generous swing, also red, looked forward to lemonade-sipping weather.

I pushed Nora up Ben's front walk and hefted the stroller two wheels at a time up the porch steps. I knocked on the oak front door, standing on my tiptoes to look through the leaded glass at the top. Ben soon appeared, taking quick strides down a hallway that cut through the center of the house.

I lifted Nora from her cocoon, and we both smiled as he opened the door.

"Welcome, Elliott girls. Come in," Ben said, moving aside to let us enter his home. He wore a brown crewneck sweater and dark jeans. I tried not to stare as I stepped into the house, but only a pulseless woman could have denied herself a second look.

The entry was simple and exactly what I would have wanted it to be. A series of framed black-and-white photos lined the center hallway, which led to a warmly lit kitchen. The house smelled clean, tidy, with a faint odor of lemon. Nothing like children. I did my best to admire the artwork from the floor, where I'd knelt to take Nora out of her snowsuit. Incidentally, this posture did nothing to flatter my figure.

"Let me take your coats," Ben offered. "You two can head left into the living room. We'll be shooting in there."

The living room was long and narrow, melting into a small dining room and a breakfast nook at the back of the house. Bach breathed sweet cello pathos into the room. The walls were painted a soft gray, trimmed at the ceiling with white crown molding. A mammoth full-length mirror in an antique silver frame hung horizontally over a side table to our left. I turned to look at our mother-daughter reflection. Our cheeks were flushed the same pink from the cold; for perhaps the first time, I could see that Nora looked like me. I smiled at her reflection.

"Hey, lovey. You look like your mommy today."

"Lucky girl," Ben said, coming up behind us.

I looked at our image of three and felt my stomach flip-flop. I turned abruptly. "Your home is beautiful, Ben," I said, moving toward the center of the room in front of a fireplace that burned white birch logs. Even the fire in Ben's house was polite, ordered. It offered warmth and light in perfect portions. My house hadn't made this much sense for years.

"Thanks," Ben said, taking stock of the room in which we stood. "It's slowly becoming home. I spend a lot of time in this room reading in front of the fire."

Slate tiles in hues of darkest blue, jade, and copper framed the fireplace. The mantle drew a simple and clean line of warm oak. Silver candles of all sizes were clustered symmetrically along the mantelpiece; they were trimmed with holly, echoing the simple wreath of berries hanging above.

I nodded in agreement. "This would be my choice spot, too. Such a lovely room. Don't you think, sweet pea?"

Nora was captivated by the dancing light of the fire. She stared without blinking, mouth open. Polka dots, fire—this girl had to get out more often.

I turned to Ben. "I hope what we're wearing is okay. You said black, right?"

Ben took in my jeans and black V-neck sweater. Nora was wearing a black velour dress with black-and-white striped tights and red Mary Janes. If I had to put down money, I'd say she was definitely the cuter.

Ben smiled. "You look great. We'll start with this and see how it goes." He moved toward a table on which several cameras waited. He picked up the smallest of the three and turned back toward us. "I'll do some candids first, and then we'll move toward the backdrop series. So just do what you do. Pretend I'm not here."

Not likely.

I put on my best Naomi Campbell and sat with Nora on the rug in front of the fireplace. We sat there for a few minutes, Nora studying the fire, first with grave seriousness and then turning to me to join in conversation.

"Geeeorseesh?"

"I know it—isn't it pretty?"

"Maamamama. Aaaaammm."

"Yes, Mama loves fire, within reason. We'll discuss fire safety when you have more teeth."

And so on and so forth while Ben clicked away. I had nearly forgotten about sucking in my stomach and was enjoying watching the light on Nora's face when Ben wrapped it up.

"Looks great, ladies. How about over to the mirror?"

This one was a little trickier, I must say. I didn't remember being so vain, but good gracious, just put me in front of a mirror while my ex-boyfriend photographs every little detail, and you'll witness a subtle but certain nervous breakdown. I tried desperately to watch Nora, which helped. She had no concerns with her thighs, which were admittedly more plus-size than mine. No worries about the drool spots on her dress or the way the fabric was just a bit too snug around the middle. She grinned like a hyena at her reflection, taking turns trying to suck the mirror and using it as a body support in order to bust a move.

I heard Ben chuckling behind his lens. "She's quite the entertainer, isn't she?"

"Gets it from her mother," I answered, making a face at Nora in the mirror. She giggled appreciatively. One of the most gratifying by-products of childbearing has to be having an in-house groupie.

Ben scanned through the last set of digital images on the screen of his camera. "Okay, girls, let's move over to the backdrop."

At the other end of the living room Ben had set up a mini-Sears' studio, only his version was both aesthetically pleasing and lacked the disgruntled employee who shakes fake flowers and stuffed frogs in the faces of miserable children. Ben's background was an expanse of white fabric suspended by two tall wrought-iron supports. The only other prop was a delicate white quilt thrown over a red wooden bench.

"I'll be right back," Ben said, restoring his camera to its place on the table. He left the room and gripped the railing as he swung up the stairs, taking them two at a time. A moment later he returned, holding a white button-down oxford shirt. "Why don't you put this on for these next few shots?"

I looked at the shirt as if it were the forbidden fruit. "Put that on?"

"Yeah, I think it will be softer, make it easier to get to where I want the photo to go."

Did he just say I'd be easier in that shirt? I shook my head slightly, trying to slow the spin. It's just a shirt, for crying out loud, I thought. Not piña coladas and getting caught in the rain. "Where shall I change?"

"The bathroom is off the main hallway, on your left." Ben took Nora from my arms. "How about you stay here with me?" he asked her, walking back toward the fire to resume hypnosis.

I started for the bathroom, my heart pounding in spite of repeated efforts to rationalize with myself. Stepping inside and locking the door, I took off my sweater. I paused and, before putting it on, buried my nose into the folds of Ben's shirt. Detergent, softener, a trace of cologne. . . . The shirt smelled like Ben. I felt momentarily disoriented, catapulted back ten years. A lifetime ago resurfaced, instantly palpable, immediate, touchable.

I stared into the bathroom mirror as I buttoned up Ben's shirt. My eyes were bright and wide, my cheeks still flushed, though no longer from the cold. I surveyed the finished product. I wore a necklace Annie'd made me buy at an art fair that summer, a delicate silver chain with a pale blue stone that floated in the crook of my collarbone. The necklace made the man's shirt look feminine and soft. So, I thought, he knows what he's doing. Just make sure you remember what *you're* doing, I reminded myself. I took a breath and opened the door.

In the living room, Ben and Nora had moved to the edge of the backdrop. Ben was watching her manhandle a lens cap. Jake should be playing with Nora this morning, I thought before I could stop myself. I swallowed. "Ready," I said.

Ben looked up and took me in with his eyes. He looked for a long moment and smiled a half smile. "You look good in my shirt," he said, eyes fixed on mine. "In fact, you look a lot better than I do in that shirt." His eyes lingered, then he broke the gaze and stood, running a hand through his hair. "Before we continue, I was thinking Nora should just be naked for these next shots."

Naked? "Um, sure," I said. "As long as she's the only one going in that direction." Good grief. Did I just say that?

Ben's mouth crept into a shy smile, and I remembered why I'd put up with him for so many years. The man could disarm a woman faster than FloJo in the open 100 meters. "Let's get started. Go ahead and sit on the bench, holding Nora on your lap."

I complied, but Nora wasn't really in a take-my-portrait mood, so we decided to roll with it. After a few awkward shots on the bench, we tossed that altogether, and Nora and I lay down on the quilt right on the hardwood. I lay on my back, throwing her into the air and making her giggle like a fiend. Nora's eyes reflected the flash; the sudden brightness startled her at first but she quickly forgot as I tickled her and sang a Raffi medley.

Five minutes in, Nora started to slow down and the giggles became infrequent.

"Do you think you can take her diaper off?" Ben asked. "I'd like to get some close-ups of you cradling her. Primitive mother and child idea."

"It might get real primitive, real fast, if I take off her diaper," I said, unsure. "Maybe we should call it a day. The morning nap draws nigh, and Nora is not one to wait quietly."

"Just a few more, I promise," Ben said, checking the flash. "I'm not quite there."

"All right," I said. "A few more."

"And Heidi," Ben added, "I'll need you to unbutton the shirt a bit farther. You know, mother-daughter skin-on-skin."

Right, I thought, blood pressure rising. Skin on skin. My fingers shook as I unbuttoned two more. Still innocent, I reminded myself. The slope isn't that slippery yet.

I stripped Nora of her skivvies, and we resumed our position on the floor. I sat cross-legged, holding naked Nora to me and feeling her breath tickle my neck. She yawned widely. The shutter on Ben's camera clicked rapid fire. I hummed a bit to Nora, shocked she was so still and cooperative. My eyes closed, feeling Ben watching us.

"That's good," he said softly, reaching over to move a strand of hair off my cheek. "This is just right."

My heart raced, eyes still closed. Nora was limp in my arms. I was considering finding a place for her to nap while Ben and I . . . um . . . caught up on old times . . .

. . . when something warm spread over my stomach.

Good Lord, please let it not be.

It was.

Nora had released all the contents of her little bladder onto Ben's shirt. I pulled her away from me, trying to cup my hand under her rump for any residual leakage.

"Ben, I'm so sorry," I wailed, looking around for a towel but seeing only the white quilt. I sat helpless, unsure of whether to hold Nora tight to Ben's shirt or over his polished hardwood.

Ben sprinted to the kitchen and returned with a roll of paper towels, a sweet but nearly useless gesture. I took a few and was blotting my front when I heard Nora grunt.

That's right. In the middle of our photo shoot, done by the light of a crackling fire and under the watchful eye of a professional photographer who happened to be unusually attractive and a former flame, my daughter had a five-alarm bowel movement all over his shirt.

I am a rock star.

Ben looked like he might puke, so I spared him the indecency of prolonging the spectacle one more minute and rushed to the bathroom, Nora in my arms. I gingerly disrobed, considered scraping off as much poop as possible and flushing it, but decided not to risk marring Ben's shining porcelain. I rolled the shirt into a ball and scrambled back into my black sweater. I did my best to clean Nora's bottom, along with her legs and halfway up her back, I might add. I hurriedly rediapered her and shoved her back into her dress, no tights. This was no time to accessorize, people.

We slunk back into the entryway, and I thrust both my arms and Nora's body into our winter gear.

"I'm really sorry, Ben," I said as he watched, ashen. Ben had never encountered infant feces, I don't believe, and he was a changed man.

He tried sounding nonchalant. "No big deal," he said with a grimace intended as a smile. "All in all, it was a great morning."

"I'll get your shirt back to you," I said, opening the front door myself. "Thanks for being so understanding."

"All right, then," he said, holding the door open for a moment, failing to hide his shudder as it closed.

I buckled Nora up in her stroller and clumped down the porch steps. I looked back to wave at Ben, but he'd already retreated to the safety of his bachelor's pad.

I turned to go, rolling my eyes at myself, my life, and my complete lack of dignity. After two blocks, my pulse had returned to a healthy rate. Maybe Nora's poop had been a timely intervention. Maybe I'd gotten too close to making a Really Big Mistake. I pushed a wailing, overtired Nora down the street and rounded the corner back home.

In any case, the moment was gone and the transformation was complete: Motherhood had officially stripped me of all class and exchanged it instead for a defecating daughter, a distant husband, and a dry cleaning bill.

Awesome.

chapter/fifteen

I held my head in my hands as the last few moments of peace dwindled away. The bell was going to ring in thirty seconds, and I wanted to milk every last one of them. The rush had been particularly draining that morning, with Jake leaving even earlier than usual and Nora even crabbier than usual. Getting her up before her inner alarm clock sounded was going to kill one of us before Christmas.

When I went in to wake her at six each morning, she'd rub her sleepy eyes and try to focus on the face above her. After a few moments, she'd smoosh her face back into her blankie and groan like a teenager awakened before high noon. I'd wait until the last possible minute to extricate her from her crib, slap on a new diaper and clothes that might or might not match, and get her into the car. I'd even begun to forgo the early-morning nursing session in favor of letting her sleep until the last minute; Rina gave her a bottle once I dropped her off. A tad more sleep for Nora, however, also meant less mother-daughter morning time. At this rate, she wouldn't even remember me when her therapist helped her sort through feelings of abandonment.

Rina, at least, exuded confidence with children, which was good since she took care of fifteen by herself in the space of nine hundred square feet. I winced each time I drove up, joining the parade of harried moms and dads dropping off their little ones before work. Rina herself always looked as unruffled as Ted Koppel, likely trying to inspire confidence in her frantic clientele. She'd stand in the doorway during the morning frenzy and smile unflinchingly come rain, sleet, or snow. "*Wilkommen, wilkommen,*" she'd intone, face paralyzed in an encouraging smile. Her daily uniform wavered only in color combinations: collared cotton shirt, stirrup pants, and bleached pair of Keds. A tightly rolled perm topped the ensemble. If she'd been famous, Rina would have been a perfect candidate to pose for a wax museum sculpture. The wardrobe, the face, the hair — the woman was unshakable.

Nora didn't seem to mind being dropped off, though she'd dabbled in the occasional clinging and predeparture panic. She was young, though, and more adaptable than her mother, so as a rule, the bottle and a pat on the head sufficed.

I, on the other hand, felt like I was nursing a hangover, though I hadn't had one of those since my freshman year of college. Back in school only three weeks and I was already longing for May dismissal. My positions as school board liaison and curriculum task force advisor had resumed in full force, and I was catching up with months of work.

My body ached, I fidgeted constantly, and worst of all, I couldn't shut off my head long enough to fall asleep at night. I'd even started fantasizing about a brief hospital stay. Imagine being able to watch trash TV while eating your meals in bed, none of which you prepared yourself, following strict orders to nap. . . . Nothing serious, mind you, just something that would lay me up for, say, five days or so. Appendicitis? Adult chicken pox? Tonsillectomy?

More likely mastitis. Out of sheer lunacy, I'd committed to keep breastfeeding Nora, even though I was away from her most of the day. This meant becoming best buddies with my breast pump. True, the pump was the Super-D-Lux Mommy Loves Me model, able to suck dry any bosom in the time it took to say, "*La Leche* rules!" And true, this was the age of enlightenment, a time when a woman should have been allowed, nay, encouraged to breastfeed until her child entered kindergarten, were it her preference.

Nevertheless, my pumping forays occurred, per Dr. Willard's embarrassed allowance, in a utility closet off the girls' locker room. There I would sit, me and my suction cups, catching snippets of gossip shared after Phys. Ed. When the coast was clear, I'd pack 'er up and head back to class, sometimes at a sprint, and store the milk in a cooler in my room.

Seriously.

With all the parenting, partnering, and pumping, I was bone tired, and even my teenage compatriots had begun to notice.

"Mrs. Elliott, you look horrible," Micah said, shaking his head as he slammed his books down on his desk. "Are you sick or something?"

"*Buenos días*, Micah," I replied, pushing myself up to stand behind my desk. "*Estoy muy cansada pero gracias por las palabras amables.*" Not sick yet, you smart aleck, but thanks for your concern. I worked hard to keep the sarcasm from creeping into my voice. He was young, male, and had the social skills of a walnut, so I really needed to cut him some slack.

The bad news was that he was not alone in the disparaging commentary. Darren held forth similar sentiments, working in the charming phrase "paler than the belly of a catfish." The girls were somewhat softer in their indictment. Jessica Collins wondered if I'd like to use her peppermint eye gel, which was *amazing* for bags under the eyes. Ana offered to get me coffee from the teachers' lounge.

"Just tired, folks," I said, momentarily too exhausted to muddle through bilingual conversation. "I'm still getting used to being back in school full-time, I guess," I said and immediately regretted it. I scanned the room, picturing the parents that went with each child, pinning down which ones would be chatting over dinner this evening with school board members or PTA presidents.

"*Trabajemos,*" I commanded. "Enough about me. Let's get to work."

Groans and gnashing of teeth, but the morning was underway. In an effort to stay awake myself, I drove those kids like a team of horses. We worked our tails off with none of the usual banter, pausing only when I would gulp down some of Ana's coffee.

The bell rang at the end of the hour, and Micah muttered on his way out, "Man, I thought popping out a kid made a person relax, Mrs. Elliott, but you're a maniac. No wonder you're tired," he said, shaking his head and *tsking* like a white-haired porch sitter.

He handed me a page torn out of his hologram spiral. "Here," he said, dangling the paper in front of me before I snatched it. "I wrote this for Claire Mueller, but don't tell. May the words of my Muse *chill you out*." He grinned and left.

I looked at the paper in my hand as I returned to my desk. "Ode, by Micah Bauer" was scrawled at the top. Drawings of guitar-wielding trolls covered the margins. In the middle of the troll-fest were these words:

You
You are
My soul, my dark, my light.

I
I know
To you I am a blight.

But listen to me;
I'm screaming for you;
Just give me a chance;
We cannot be through.

Yeah, yeah, oh, oh, oh.

We
Could be
So sweet, so pure, so true.

Please
Just see
My hands, they reach for you.

You know you need me.
You know you need me.
You know you need me.
Oh, oh yeah, it's so true.

Wow. I hoped Micah would have better luck with Claire.

I collapsed into my chair. Only six periods to go, I thought, laying my head on my desk for the few moments before my next class entered.

I made it through third and fourth hour and was fighting a nap halfway through my planning period when there was a sharp rap at the door. I whipped up my head, flinched at the whiplash, and barked, "It's open!"

General McMinn flung open the door and poked her head into the room. "Heidi," she said, eyebrows arched, "your baby-sitter just called."

My heart sank and I leaped to my feet. "Is everything all right?"

"You'd better call her." McMinn pursed her lips. "She said your little girl has some sort of rash." With that, the Minister of Compassion let the door slam behind her.

I flew close behind, speeding wildly down the foreign language hall and through the science wing before veering off to the teachers' lounge. After hurtling toward the phone table at the back of the room, I tapped into an outside line and dialed Rina's number, needing to do it three times before I got it right.

My hands were shaking. Sweat beaded at the nape of my neck. Nora has some sort of rash? I thought, listening to Rina's phone ring once, twice. Do measles start as a rash? What about polio? Lyme disease? Nora, along with most children in the U.S. living in the twenty-first century, had been vaccinated for two of these things and hadn't seen a mosquito for four months, but that gave me absolutely no comfort. I panted into the phone, immersed in panic.

Somewhere in my head, I realized the room of gossiping teachers had gone silent and was watching Psycho Mom handle her first parenting crisis, some of them thrilled to have such a delicious diversion in their day. There was a whole group of sloth teachers who, I swear, were paid to sit in the lounge while their classes ate paint off the walls in boredom. These people loved videos, crossword puzzles, word searches. In fact, Mr. Drummond, one of the math teachers . . .

"Hello?" Rina answered in her thick German accent. Not to be ruffled by a morbidly ill seven-month-old, Rina, predictably, sounded perfectly calm.

"Rina. It's Heidi. What's going on?"

"I am most fine, tank you. And you, Missus Elliott?"

"What? Fine, fine. You called. Nora. What's going on?" I paced the room as far as the phone would reach.

"Nora has a rash on her abdominals, Missus Elliott. I do not know its origin, but because of the other *kinder*, I will ask you to please come and pick up, tank you."

"Of course I'll come," I said. The Lounge Rats twittered with delight. "Can you tell me more about the rash, Rina? I mean, is it bright red? Does it itch? Are there bumps?" I stopped myself. What was I, an MD? And did I really trust Rina to be thorough, anyway? I mean, nice lady, but the fact that she'd even noticed a rash among fourteen other *kinder* was astonishing. "Listen," I said, "I'll be right there. Just hang tight, and tell Nora Mommy's on her way."

I hung up without waiting for a reply. I got another dial tone and punched in Jake's office line and then his cell. He answered neither, and I didn't wait to leave a message. As I turned to leave, there was lots of demonstrative rustling and exaggerated throat clearing. Mrs. Sniff, the ninth grade science teacher, said in much too loud a voice, "So, Bob, what were you saying about your hunting trip this weekend?"

Mr. Drummond giggled uncomfortably. Some sloths are better liars than others.

I rolled my eyes as I left, hoping every last one of the Rats saw me do it.

℮ ℈ ℮

After a quick stop in my room, I locked the door and sprinted toward the school office. I pulled on my coat, swinging the door open with my hip. "Mrs. McMinn, I'm going to have to pick up my daughter at day care."

The Iron Maiden raised her penciled brows, not looking up from her computer screen. "Well, you'll need to speak with Dr. Willard about that." She swiveled over to her phone and pushed a button. "Dr. Willard, Heidi Elliott to see you." Pregnant pause, and then, "She says she's leaving for the day." McMinn replaced the phone in its cradle and said with feigned sweetness, "Take a seat, Heidi. He'll be right out."

I did not, of course, take a seat, but spent the next interminable minutes shifting my weight in front of McMinn's desk, which she most certainly did not appreciate. Undeterred by the pointed stares and exasperated sighing, I stayed put. Listen, I couldn't possibly sit and read some back issue of *Reader's Digest* when my daughter could be showing the first signs of Asian bird flu.

Dr. Willard sauntered out of his office and came to stand in front of me, arms crossed over his chest. "Heidi, what seems to be the problem?" The image of his hand on Stillwell's at Maurizio's flashed through my head.

"Nora's sick," I gushed. "I need to go pick her up. Sub plans for the afternoon are on my desk."

I saw McMinn and Willard exchange a knowing glance.

"I see, I see," said Dr. Willard, rolling up and down on the balls of his Pygmy feet. "Yes, well, we'll see what we can do about a sub. And you understand this would be counted as one of your three personal days for the year."

I nodded dumbly. He looked at the clock. "Only ten minutes until the start of sixth hour." He thought long and hard, clearly a difficult combination.

"So, I'll just go, then," I said, heading toward the door.

"Heidi, heh, heh. I'm afraid you won't be able to leave until we've found a replacement to teach your classes."

"I'm sorry?" McMinn had begun to type like a wild woman at her keyboard. I searched Willard's face for mercy. "Can't you ask someone with a planning period to fill in until the sub arrives? Maybe Rachel Davis or another first-year who'd be willing to pitch in?" Visions of a flushed Nora, covered in a Calcutta-level rash, tormented me as I spoke.

"Now, Heidi," he said, cocking his fleshy head to one side and talking as one would to someone who'd suffered severe head injuries. "Would it really be fair to punish your colleagues just because you had a baby?" He smiled like Santa, absently patting his own bowlful of jelly. "They need their planning period just as you need yours. I'm sorry your daughter is sick, but she's in competent hands, and we have a school to run." He shrugged as if to say, Tough luck, sweetie, but I warned you.

I felt my panic rising out of control. "How about Ms. Stillwell?" I blurted. "She's at home, right? She could come?"

Bad move. Dr. Willard's face turned to stone. "Why don't you let me take care of that?" he snapped. "We'll let you know when you are released to go." With that, he barreled back into his office, clicking the door shut behind him.

I looked at McMinn, hoping for some female solidarity, some assuaging comment that would let me know this happened all the time, that Nora would be okay, and that a sub would be there within minutes. She didn't even look up. Her Great Oz had spoken.

I slunk out of the office and was swept up into the human tide of passing period. I pushed and pulled my way back to my classroom, still reeling from my conversation with Dr. Willard. Isn't this illegal? I wondered. Some sort of discrimination? Unlawful prejudice against a working mother? Nora's little face crowded my head, and I felt tears stinging my eyes.

Please, God, I prayed. Let someone come soon so I can go to Nora. And help her to be okay. I'm sorry I only come to You when I want something. I promise I'll work on that. Just please . . . My prayer drifted off as I unlocked the classroom door, pulled off my coat, draped it over my chair. The students of sixth period jostled each other, eking out the moments before submitting to fifty-five minutes in their seats.

I spend my days taking care of other people's children, I thought, watching them laugh, talk, flirt as the bell began to chime. I should not be here, I agonized, and pulled myself up to start class.

e ව e

"Nora Elliott." A tall, mannish nurse read the name off Nora's chart and looked up expectantly. I caught her eye as I rose with Nora, her car seat, diaper bag, and my purse. I shuffled toward Man-Woman like a fully loaded burro, passing rows of frazzled mothers and their sick charges.

"You may put your things in the exam room while we go to the weighing station," said Man-Woman, sizing up my bundle but not going so far as to help. This was unfortunate, as she had biceps the size of my head and could have twirled Nora's car seat on her index finger, Globetrotter style.

Nora buried her face into my neck as we headed to the scale. She was warm and lethargic, not even tempted by the life-size poster of Big Bird hanging on the wall. I stripped her down to her diaper, exposing the raised red bumps on her belly, and lay her on the cold metal scale, which made her eyes flicker open and spark with question marks. She took a sharp breath of surprise and then let out a serious wail.

"I know, sweetums, it's a little chilly, isn't it?" asked Man-Woman, not unkindly but with the finesse of a garbage truck outside your door at six in the morning. She moved quickly to get Nora's height from a measure attached to the scale and then straightened up to her full six foot three. "All done, honey bear. Back to the exam room."

I followed obediently, trying to shield naked Nora from the draft as I walked. We sat down in a blue chair. The walls mocked us with posters of animals and lollipop wallpaper. The room reeked of hand gel and bleach, which was good considering the plethora of other options.

The nurse began her inquisition, eyes glued to her clipboard. "Symptoms?"

"Rash and fever. She's been acting very lethargic this afternoon."

"How long have the symptoms been present?"

"Just today."

"Any other complaints?"

"Um, not that I know of. She can't really complain yet." Did she just roll her eyes under that mullet?

"Nora your only child?"

"Yes."

"Day care?"

Gulp. "Yes."

"Full-time?"

"Yes." Why don't you just slit my wrists for me?

"Any smokers in the house?"

"No." Yessssss! One point for me!

"All right, Dr. Holland will be in shortly. Keep Nora undressed so he can take a look."

"Thank you," I mumbled, cuddling Nora to me for protection from any more questioning. What a world, I thought bitterly. I work for years to educate myself, cultivate my career, shine my light for the Rachel Davises of the world as I fight against the proverbial glass ceiling. Then, when I have a child, fulfilling not only my personal life but also my duty as a procreator of the human race, I'm blamed for her illness because I can't take care of her full-time because I'm busy being a light for the glass-ceiling crowd. Can't win, I thought, rocking Nora in my arms.

There was a soft knock at the door. Dr. Holland smiled at us over his glasses as he entered. His face was ruddy and handsome, even with his nearly seventy years. He wore a calf-length white coat with his name inscribed, the color of the coat a match to his thinning hair. "Hello, Elliott girls," he said merrily. I'd clicked my heels with glee when I got a spot in Dr. Holland's burgeoning pediatric practice. Springdale was so grossly underserved by pediatricians, a parent nearly had to audition with test scores, IQ work-ups, and a musical routine to get a coveted place in a good practice.

Dr. Holland sat down across from me. "Nora's not feeling well today, are you, sweetheart?" His blue eyes crinkled with compassion. I thought I might burst into tears.

"She has a rash," I said, showing him the red bumps.

Nora remained limp in my arms, only occasionally opening her eyes to look at Dr. Holland. She turned her face into my chest and moaned as Dr. Holland examined first her abdomen, then her throat, eyes, and ears. He used his stethoscope to listen to her heart and closed his eyes to hear her breathe. He made a few notes on Nora's chart and then sat down.

"You may dress her, Heidi."

I pushed Nora's arms through her pink and purple shirt and looked at Dr. Holland for his diagnosis.

"Heart and lungs sound good. Her throat is a little red and her right eye is tearing. But there's no sign of an ear infection, and her fever is still low-grade." He shrugged. "So I think we'll just watch the rash and the fever and assume it's some sort of virus that is making her uncomfortable. Has she had any trouble sleeping?"

"I don't know yet," I said, pulling on Nora's purple velour pants. "This all started today."

"Watch her sleeping and her appetite," Dr. Holland said, writing as he talked. "Make sure she remains hydrated and call us if her fever either doesn't respond to medication or goes above 104 degrees."

"One hundred four! Aren't humans dead by then?" I realized my hands were shaking as I tried to pull Nora's socks over her toes. "And what do you mean it's a virus? Does that mean no antibiotics?"

"Antibiotics are useless for viral infections. Tylenol or ibuprofen should relieve most of her discomfort," Dr. Holland said with patience. I had a feeling I was not the first high-strung mother who'd crossed his path. "The rash is likely a by-product of the fever, so just keep an eye on it and let us know if it changes or gets worse."

"How long will it last?" I meant the virus, though the next eighteen years loomed in front of me full of worry and angst for not being able to fix everything for my little girl.

"A typical virus runs its course within seven to ten days." Dr. Holland was watching as I fumbled with Nora's winter coat. "Heidi," he said softly, "you're doing everything you need to be doing. You're a good mother."

"She goes to day care," I blurted. Don't cry, don't cry, I pleaded with myself. The zipper on Nora's coat blurred.

Dr. Holland smiled. "As do many, many well-adjusted children in this country. Piling on the guilt will not help Nora get well any faster, nor will it make you a better mother."

I nodded, biting my lip.

Dr. Holland reached over to help me with the zipper. "Nora's thriving, Heidi. She's gaining weight, and overall she's a happy, healthy little girl. Sick kids can be stressful, but it's an unavoidable part of parenting. You'll do just fine, and Nora will be better in no time at all."

I sniffed and took the Kleenex he offered with a meek "Thanks."

He rose to go. "Give us a call if you have any questions. We have someone available at all times of the day." He patted me on the shoulder and looked down at Nora, who'd succumbed to a restless sleep. "Feel better soon, Nora." He touched her lightly on her head and went out the door. I heard him slide Nora's chart into its cubby outside the exam room and walk down the carpeted hallway to his next miserable patient and more miserable mother.

I sat for a moment holding my sleeping daughter. The high tide of emotion that had bombarded me since Rina's call escaped without recourse, and I waited through the flood of silent, hot tears, letting them wash my face and Nora's coat. My head reeled with sub instructions, calls to Dr. Willard, contingency plans for missing a few days of work. Though I knew staying home with my sick child was a no-brainer, I still couldn't help but cringe when I remembered the knowing look that had passed between McMinn and Willard. Just as he'd so obnoxiously expected, I thought. Well, sir, sometimes mommies have a wee wittle hard time being sixty places at once and doing any of them well. I hope you're happy, Dr. W.

I blotted my eyes with one of the clinic's scratchy tissues. I looked down at Nora, her face flushed with fever and further reddened by the insane mother who had prematurely swaddled her up in a six-layer winter coat. Nora's eyes flickered, betraying her flight through hard sleep. I kissed her face, feeling the warmth of the fever through her little cheek. With careful hands, I nestled her into the car seat and propped the door open with my foot.

Shouldering our load once again, I headed out of the exam room, past the reception desk and lobby of snot-clogged kids. On my way out to the car, I left a voice mail for Jake. "Nora's sick," I said after the beep. "Dr. Holland thinks it's a virus. I'll stay home but could lose my job. Though I might just be happy about that at this point. He said I'm a good mom but I don't believe him. And can you pick up something for dinner? Anything is fine. Nothing sounds good. Thanks."

I slouched into the driver's seat, vaguely acknowledging I'd just left a message in Swahili. I checked Nora in the rearview mirror. Her cheeks drooped with sleep, her head propped at a right angle against the side of her seat. I turned the key in the ignition and we headed home.

chapter/sixteen

Through a heavy veil of sleep, I felt someone watching me.

I opened my eyes partway, focusing slowly on a cockeyed view of our front yard. Freezing rain hit the window, the drops tapping lightly on the glass. I was curled on my side in a fetal position, clutching the baby monitor to my belly. Our striped comforter swallowed me whole.

Annie sat at the foot of the bed. "Hi," she said softly, brow creased, eyes bright with concern.

I sat up in stages, finally propping my upper body against the headboard behind me.

"Hi," I said, rubbing my eyes and yawning.

The monitor was silent. I looked at the clock. Nora had been sleeping for three hours; I wasn't sure how long I'd napped with her.

"Why are you here?" I asked, squinting in the afternoon light.

"Jake called me at the office," Annie said. She was still in her scrubs, hair held back by a black clip. "He said he got a really bizarre phone message from you and wanted to make sure you were okay. He couldn't get away from the store until after five thirty, but I finished early today, so I headed over to check on you." She rubbed my foot through the rumpled comforter. "You okay?"

"I'm fine," I said, just a little huffy. "Nora's sick, so I took her to the doctor. Willard was a complete jerk about letting me leave, which threw me into a funk. Worrying about Nora made me exhausted. I must have fallen asleep after I put her in bed." I stared at the quiet monitor, watching the little red noise lights remain steady.

"How about a cup of tea?" Annie asked, heading to the kitchen without waiting for a response.

Annie was into tea. It made her feel British or something. She had collected twenty-seven teapots and was constantly making me try her latest favorite blends, like jasmine honey-suckle or mango chutney madness. I didn't have the heart to warn her she'd only find crumpled-up Liptons in the recesses of my cupboard.

I shuffled to the kitchen, feeling my head awaken before my body. I wondered who had subbed for me that afternoon, if someone might still be at the school office. Dr. Willard would need to be notified of my plans to stay home the next couple of days. There went my two days of paid leave. I could just imagine Iron Maiden's clucking about my fall from grace.

"Honey or sugar?" Annie asked, putting a cup of water to heat in the microwave. She must have wisely discerned I didn't own a teapot. "Lemon?"

"Straight-up black, please," I said, lowering myself into a kitchen chair. I took stock of my kitchen: dirty breakfast dishes in the sink, garbage can full to brimming, vase of dried and brittle flowers on the table. "Sorry my house is such a mess."

"Give me a break." Annie rolled her eyes. She may have been a perfectionist, but she was patient with us right-brained slobs.

The microwave beeped and Annie exchanged the hot cup for a cold one. She punched some buttons and the turntable started rotating again. She dropped a tea bag in the steaming water and placed it in front of me.

I cupped my hands around the mug, feeling the warmth sink like hot silk into my cold fingers. "Why am I so ridiculously tired?" I moaned, letting the tea's moist warmth bathe my closed eyelids.

"Because you're trying to do everything, which is physically impossible." Annie dipped her little finger into the other cup and, satisfied, submerged the Lipton. She took a seat across from me at the kitchen table.

"Well, that's pathetic," I said, grimacing at my own sorry state. "I'm a teacher, a wife, and a mom. That's it. Not CEO of a Fortune 500 company, not the president of the United States or even a cabinet member. And I mother only one child. I should be thankful for my easy life!" I checked myself and lowered my voice, not wanting to wake Nora. "My problems aren't even problems, but all I can do is feel exhausted. Pathetic."

I took a huge gulp of my tea and scalded my mouth.

Annie stayed silent, sipped her tea like the queen of England. In the absence of sound, I heard my outburst replay on a continuous loop.

"One of my students told me I look horrible," I sulked.

"You don't look horrible," Annie said carefully. "But you do look tired, run-down."

She seemed like she wanted to say more, so I said, "What?"

"Pardon?"

"What do you want to say? I know that look. That look says, 'I want to say something else but she might not like it.' Just say it. I can take it."

Annie looked into her teacup for a while, screwing up her mouth like when we were kids and nearing the end of a cutthroat game of Monopoly. "I was just thinking that maybe you should consider taking time off from teaching. You know, staying at home."

I looked at her incredulously. "You've got to be kidding."

She spoke quickly. "I'm not kidding. Just think about it. You could spend all day with Nora, taking care of her. The first few years are so important, aren't they? I mean, isn't there research about the crucial first five years? Something about preventing ADD or drug abuse? And Jake makes enough to support your family, right? You couldn't exactly buy out Nordstrom or anything, but—"

"Annie," I cut her off. My face was red, I was sure, and it had nothing to do with the tea. "You're insulting me."

A look of bewilderment crossed her face. "What?"

"You, the only female dentist in town, the one who made a career out of overachieving, you want to suggest that I can't handle it? I can't take the heat, so I should just stay home for a few years until things get a little easier and Nora can make her own peanut butter sandwiches?"

"Heidi—"

I shook my head. "I can't believe you think I can't cut it." I looked down to hide my disgust. "I may not be a freakin' medical professional, but I am very good at what I do, and I'll figure out how to do what millions of women do every single day: work, pay bills, be a wife, and raise a child. It cannot possibly be this difficult." I slumped in my chair, sipping noisily from my cup.

Annie sat, chagrined. She let her mane out of the clip and ran slender fingers through her hair. I looked at her face. Her eyes showed the wound I'd inflicted. Though she could body slam most men with her wiry frame, Annie was not one to fight with words. I could see I'd hurt her, but I did nothing to make things better. My pride was limping and I was busy nursing it back to health.

Annie cleared her throat. "Well. I didn't mean to insult you, Heidi. It was only a suggestion."

"Thanks for the suggestion, Doc, but I've got it together." I avoided her gaze.

We heard the front door open and Jake stomping snow off his shoes. He entered the kitchen with a question mark on his face. "How's it going?" He walked over to the table, taking a seat beside me. "Are you okay?" I could smell the takeout he'd deposited on the counter.

"I'm fine," I said in my best Tom Brokaw, capable and diagnostic. "Just tired. We'll see how Nora's faring when she wakes from her nap." While I gave Jake a summary of the doctor visit, Annie listened without a word. She tipped her cup to finish off the tea.

Jake looked at Annie and said, "Thanks for checking up on them."

"No problem," Annie said, rising from her chair and going to rinse her cup under the faucet. "I need to get going. Call me later, Heidi, and let me know how Nora's doing." She gave a quick wave to Jake and left, never looking in my direction.

Jake watched me, waiting for an explanation of why the woman who usually takes no fewer than thirty minutes to say good-bye could leave in such a rush. I got up to dump the rest of my tea in the sink.

"How are you feeling?" Jake asked, watching me from his chair.

"I said I'm fine," I snapped. "Why does everyone keep asking me that as if I've just donated a spleen? Nora's the one who is sick. I'm fine, just tired. Like most women in America, probably." I closed my eyes, rubbing the back of my neck with both hands. "Thanks for picking up dinner," I said more quietly. "I need to call Dr. Willard and tell him I'll be home for the next couple of days."

I felt Jake's eyes on me as I left the kitchen.

In the old days, Jake never would have let me escape the room after a mini-tirade like that. In the old days, he would have insisted that we talk through whatever was really bugging me and come to some sort of resolution. In the old days, we had make-up sex.

But, I admitted to myself, these were not the old days.

I clicked shut the bedroom door and sat down to call my boss.

e ᴐ e

Though her body needed it more than ever, sleep eluded Nora that night. The digital clock in the nursery mocked me with the incremental passage of time. Hours melted into hours, each of them witness to a baby fighting the sleep she craved and a mother fighting delirium. Once we passed the three o'clock mark, I gave up being angry that Jake slept soundly through Nora's cries, and I succumbed to a night on the nursery floor. Anger maintenance required too much energy at that point.

Our longest stretch of sleep came at the end of the battle, between five and eight that morning. Three hours of rest under her belt, Nora woke fussy but finally with an appetite. I felt rather fussy myself and found myself missing the prospect of escaping to a room of adolescents.

"Morning, sweet pea," I murmured in my daughter's ear. I could feel the fever rising off her cheek. "It's just the two of us today."

Nora hid her face in my neck as I brought her to the rocker for a made-to-order breakfast. God bless a day without the D-Lux. "I'm on meal duty all day, sweet girl," I said as I stroked Nora's forehead. "Rina has the day off."

At the mention of Rina's name, Nora's eyes fluttered open and then closed in slow motion over cloudy eyes. I would need to give her another dose of Motrin as soon as breakfast was over.

After declining a dessert of sliced peaches, Nora sat with me on my bed. I tucked my legs into a pretzel position and held Nora as we rocked slowly back and forth. She was content to inhale and exhale, her hand on my neck as I hummed. The Motrin began to settle into her system; I could hold her without breaking out into a sweat myself.

Fever must have remained, however, because my singing calmed her. While pregnant with Nora, my ears had perked during a morning talk show segment on ways to calm a cranky

infant. When the baby soothing "expert" had mentioned singing to your baby to help her relax, she'd added quickly, "But,
of course, only sing to your baby if you have a *pleasant* voice.
Don't want to further upset your little duck sounding like a
bullfrog." At that, she and the plastic host had thrown back
their heads in automaton laughter.

On behalf of all the bullfrogs in the mothering world, I
disagreed with Plastic and Expert. Just as Nora cast no judg-
ment on my interpretation of the Hustle, she liked my voice.
I sang with heart, for crying out loud. In the words of Paula
Abdul, I made songs my *own*. Indeed, I was proof that one
truly can bounce back from pointed comments made by
elementary choir teachers.

Okay, and junior high and high school.

Nora listened as I made my way through "Edelweiss,"
sounding only slightly less sonorous than Captain von Trapp.
She looked up, completely relaxed in my arms. I stopped singing and put my cheek to her cheek. My eyes were closed but I
knew what she looked like, drifting into sleep, her breathing
soft and regular. I kept my cheek against hers, feeling rivulets
of my tears wet our faces.

She slept and I rocked, letting myself feel for the first time
how much I'd missed her.

℮ ℗ ℮

For most people, three days of quarantine with a sick kid was
not a vacation. It was Tuesday afternoon when Nora got sick,
and I stayed home with her for the rest of the week. That girl
was wiped out, and I wasn't about to take her back to Rina's

until she had the strength to hold her own in the day care jungle. Besides, to my surprise, I liked being back home.

That was not to say there wasn't a readjustment period. The first day, I paced while Nora slept. After detailing sub plans for the rest of the week, I called school to make sure the sub was faring well. I even made dinner early. When I was halfway through color coordinating my soup cans, I paused, cream of mushroom in hand, and realized I could stop.

It was okay to stop.

Three full minutes were spent musing on that revelation before I finally put the cream of mushroom back on the shelf, closed the pantry door, and sat down on the couch.

That was when the fun began.

For starters, I took a nap. That's right, a nap, right in the middle of sixth period. Absolutely glorious. It did take a half hour to turn off my brain, but I did it. Three days in a row, and it was amazing.

I also wrote a letter to my great-aunt Leila with a pen, on real stationery, and mailed it the same day. I hoped Auntie Leila wouldn't experience any adverse effects to her weak heart upon receiving handwritten correspondence from her negligent niece, but I did feel like preprison Martha Stewart for a shining moment.

The shift into low gear also allowed me to reacquaint myself with my daughter. I watched Nora play for twenty minutes at a time, tickled by her intrigue with a wooden spoon or a pocket mirror. Perhaps I saw what I wanted to see, but I thought she liked having me around again. Or maybe she could sense my slower pace and was happy to have this version instead of Harried Morning Mom and Grumpy Nighttime Mom.

I became adept at ignoring the growing pile of laundry and only occasionally let my mind drift back to my real life and the work I'd face Monday. Dinners were simple but tasty enough; I only called Jake once for takeout, and I almost enjoyed cooking again.

My utopia flagged because Nora felt horrible, unequivocally so until Friday and considerably so until Sunday morning. Her heightened need for me granted total freedom from guilt for missing work, even with Willard's grumblings and a bulging inbox. The decision to be home with Nora those few days was a black-and-white one for me, and I savored the decisiveness. I hadn't felt so clear in purpose since I'd voted against Dole in 1996.

Purpose felt good.

Even Willow noticed my change of attitude when I saw her at Moms' Group Wednesday evening. After Molly adjourned, I stayed for virgin eggnogs and gingerbread cookies. I chatted with Laura Ingalls, who wanted to know if I'd like to join her in a Christmas fundraiser called Baby Jesus Aerobics. After bowing out due to a slightly exaggerated high school track injury, I talked with Willow as we pulled on hats and gloves.

"You look rosy, Heidi," Willow noted with a twinkle in her eyes. "Lots of honeymoon kissing lately?"

To be honest, I hadn't thought much about Jake the last few days, much less planted any on him. He'd been at the store until late, and I was busy playing Nurse Nightingale meets Zen Homemaker.

"Actually," I said, "I've been home with a sick little girl this week."

"Oh, no," Willow said, worry pulling her mouth into a frown. "Is Nora okay?"

"She will be," I said, buttoning my coat. "We're doing well, considering." I chuckled. "Irony of ironies, I haven't felt this rested in weeks."

Willow nodded. "I remember wishing for a break from the madness." She raised an eyebrow. "Though I don't recall sick kids being much of a respite."

"It is strange," I agreed. We passed through the Langdons' front door and headed for our parked cars. "I'm not saying the house is clean or I've been productive at all. But as you said, I am rosier. That has to count for something, right? Isn't there a Rosy Index that cancels out details like vacuuming and professional advancement?"

Willow smiled wryly and said, "My dear, if you have already learned that lesson at such a tender age, I salute you and wish you Godspeed. The Rosy Index. Excellent idea and I hope you don't forget about it entirely come Monday morning."

I thought about Willow's words on the way home, first that Willow thought I was at a "tender age," when I'd felt down-right elderly as of late. And second, that I could be on the brink of knowing something important enough that Willow, knower of Big Life Lessons, would salute me.

Still tallying up the week's events, I wondered if I should be more worried about the romance drought in the Elliott house. I hadn't heard much about Jana Van Fleet lately; in fact, Jake could have even finished the condo job by now.

Maybe it was safe to try to patch things up, initiate a prebaby level of lovin'.

I pulled into our driveway, checking the Rosy Index in my rearview mirror. I hurried up the front path, light on my feet and ready to pay new attention to my husband.

The front door's creak broke the silence of our house. All the lights were out. The kitchen night-light cut a dim path through darkness. I found Jake sleeping soundly on his side of the bed. I thought of waking him, snuggling up to see what might happen. After a short deliberation, though, I wavered in my resolve. Instead of spooning, I crept to the closet and tugged out my comfy pajamas. I kept the bathroom light off while I brushed my teeth, slid between the sheets, and settled for dropping a kiss on Jake's forehead.

He didn't even stir.

chapter/seventeen

By Sunday night, Nora was running at about 98 percent. Her fever had broken Friday morning, and the rash had disappeared. Her eyes had cleared; she was babbling to her toys again. The only residual effect of her illness was the lingering need to hibernate. She slept most of the weekend. One more night of catch-up sleep and we'd be back into the swing of things.

With Nora better and work responsibilities squared away for the time being, I turned my attention to the home front. We were completely out of toilet cleaner, paper towels, Windex, and laundry detergent. The only food in the house had either been processed and frozen in Arkansas in 1989 or was green and crumbled at the touch.

The time had come for a shopping trip.

Jake left after a dinner of frozen pizza for a Sunday night poker game with Rob and some other work buddies. He'd told me not to wait up, so I hoped to do a few errands, run a bath, and get to bed early, anticipating the resumed chaos of a new work week starting bright and early the next morning. I called Lauren at the last minute to see if she could come put Nora to bed early and stay while I left for a couple of hours.

"Of course, Mrs. Elliott," she said, probably packing her babysitter's safety pack as we spoke. "I'll have my mother bring me right over." I thought I heard her smile "ding" like in a spearmint gum commercial before she hung up.

Fifteen minutes later Lauren was on my doorstep. Nora smiled and kicked to see her, and I had to admit, Lauren did inspire confidence. Slinging her safety pack over an armchair, Lauren held out her hands to take Nora. Nora squealed and slung her body into Lauren's embrace.

"Hey, there, little one," she said, and ushered Nora over to a pile of books. After brief instructions and a sly kiss on Nora's head, I tiptoed toward the front door and opened it without drawing even a look from Nora. Lauren raised her eyebrows in farewell, winking conspiratorially as I slipped out.

ℰ ℈ ℰ

"Cold night to be standing out here," I said to the Salvation Army man outside of Target.

He chuckled. "Sure is, ma'am, but at least I have a house to warm up in when I'm through."

I folded up a ten and shimmied it into the red bucket.

"Thank you and Merry Christmas," he said and resumed his bell ringing.

The bright, sterile lights of Target greeted me. I blinked into them as I stamped the cold off my body. After corralling a shiny red cart, I scanned the aisles for cleaning supplies, taking a detour in holiday decorations. In a moment of honesty, I slapped two wreaths into my cart, admitting to myself that I would not have time to make my own this or any other year before Nora turned twenty-five and lived out of state. Three days home with my child had reminded me what was important. My glue gun was staying in the closet.

I slid an econo-size detergent off the shelf and into my cart. While I consulted my list and made a wide U-turn toward the pharmacy, my cell phone rang. I fished it out of my purse during the third ring and answered without checking the caller ID. "Hello?"

"Heidi. I'm so glad I got you."

"Ben?" Had I given him my cell number? My heart rate shifted into high gear.

"Listen, I hope you don't mind that I got your cell from your babysitter. By the way, is she abnormally *ancient* for her age? She actually used the word 'delighted.'"

I giggled. "That's Lauren. She's a fifty-year-old trapped in a nubile teenage body. But she's an amazing babysitter."

"Plenty of time to knit and darn socks after the kiddies are in bed."

"Now, be nice," I said, the smile staying on my face. Such lovely banter we have, I thought. Effortless compared to other recent patterns of male-female communication in my life. . . .

"Listen, Heidi," he said. "I'd be forever indebted if you'd stop by my house sometime tonight. Lauren said you were running errands? If that can wait, I need you to come over. My deadline is tomorrow, and it just occurred to me that my layout needs a photo of you, by yourself." I heard him tinkering with something in the background. "The photos with Nora turned out great, but the set is incomplete. You're more than just a mom. No offense," he added hastily.

"None taken," I said. "I forget it sometimes myself."

"So you'll come?"

"Tonight?" My watch said nine thirty. I was one of the only shoppers left in Target. "Isn't it kind of late?"

"Not for me. Jake's out with the boys, right?"

Wow, he'd done his homework. "Yeah, he told me not to wait up."

"Perfect. Can you be here in ten minutes?"

What about the grocery store? "I'll be right over." I hung up and checked out, postponing the food run and resigning the Elliott family to one more night of preservatives. After all, how many women get called out of discount store shopping to be photographed?

Things like this don't happen every day, I reasoned, and started toward Ben's bungalow.

ℰ ꙅ ℰ

He was ready when I arrived.

"Hi," he said with a grin, holding the door open. It takes a real man to wear pink, and Ben got it done in a broken-in corduroy button-down. His hair was tousled, eyes dark and sparking. My stomach flipped at the smell of his cologne. I stepped past him and inside. He took my coat and I kicked off my snowy shoes, feeling the cold of the hardwood floor through my socks.

Ben led me into the living room aglow with candlelight. Candles on the mantelpiece, candles on the bookshelves, the coffee table, even on the floor. The effect was spellbinding, the suffused light softening edges and teasing the darkness.

"This is beautiful," I whispered.

He said nothing but left the room. I watched the light dance, captivated, until he returned holding a glass of red wine.

"Thanks for coming on such short notice," he said as I took the glass. "I owe you one."

His face studied mine as I sipped the wine carefully. Slowly, slowly, I told myself, already feeling woozy from my surroundings. I switched the glass to my left hand when I realized I was fingering my wedding band.

Ben went to get his camera and, after a few moments, asked me to take a seat. This time there was no backdrop, no props—just his classic, astronomically expensive furniture cradling a rough-hewn coffee table. A fire crackled in the fireplace, the amber light reaching long fingers into the cozy room.

I sat in a Mission-style chair trimmed in black leather, first moving aside the chenille throw Ben had draped over the back. I looked down at my clothes, glad I'd worn the merino sweater that complemented the green in my eyes. My new jeans lifted and gave in all the right places, joining in the celebration of being only one size away from pre-Nora measurements.

"I hope what I'm wearing will work," I said, feeling my mouth pull up into a half smile. "I promise I won't need to dry clean any of your personal effects after tonight."

Ben smiled and shook his head. "You can keep that shirt, by the way. Neither it nor I will ever be the same."

I sipped my wine, aware again of how different our lives were at this point. Perhaps that was what felt so nice. . . .

He photographed me watching him. The light flickered throughout the room, casting warm shadows into corners, making a cocoon of the small space. After a while, I shut my eyes, drinking in the final stillness of a beautifully quiet week.

"Nora was sick this week," I murmured, eyes closed.

Ben didn't answer, the shutter still clicking. I opened my eyes; he shot a few more. My head was spinning but not because of the Merlot. How exhilarating it was to be studied, admired. You're on dangerous ground here, I heard deep inside myself. I took another drink.

After a few moments, he lowered his camera. "That's it," he said. "Exactly what I wanted." He shook his head, looking down at the floor. "You're really beautiful, Heidi."

I gulped. I *love* these jeans. "Thank you," I said, locking my eyes with his. I could feel my heart pounding and hoped he couldn't hear it from where he was, which was not very far away.

"I mean," he continued, searching my face, "you were always beautiful, but I think motherhood has made you even more so."

Good gracious, did this man know how to talk to a woman or what?

I licked my lips, hoping the gloss I'd applied before getting out of my car was shimmering in the candlelight. I made them pout a bit, going for a little Angelina Jolie.

"Heidi," Ben said, clasping his hands in front of him, "I've been wanting to ask you something."

Look alive! Look alive! This is it!

I made my eyes as huge as possible, working now for super-model meets Bambi. He's been wanting to ask me something!

He's going to say it, I thought, my pulse quickening anew. He's going to force us to confront the unmistakable chemistry between us, admit his undying, unrequited love, ask me to come away with him to Tahiti, or at least as far as Palm Springs.

I leaned toward him and waited, breathless.

"I hope this doesn't catch you off guard," he said.

"Not at all," I nearly gushed. I *knew* he still loved me. I'd known it since that first day back on our porch, by the way he wanted me to wear his shirt. Of course, I could never leave Jake and Nora, but still, he made me feel beautiful, wanted. . . .

"I was just wondering . . ." Ben sat forward in his chair across from me. ". . . what you'd think . . ." He took my hands in his. His eyes were fixated on my face. I was watching his mouth. ". . . if I were to . . ." Yes? ". . . ask Annie out for dinner."

I stared. "Annie?"

"I know," he said, rushing to defend himself. "It may sound a bit odd, what with the history between the two of us." He smiled sheepishly. "Though, of course, that was eons ago. We were children." He shook his head, laughing appreciatively at the silliness of it all.

"Children, yes," I mumbled. Annie?

"So, do you think she'd consider it?" He looked at me, hope shining from his exasperatingly chiseled face. He shrugged. "I guess seeing you with a family, a little girl, has made me think more seriously about settling down myself, really for the first time in my life. And when I saw Annie at the café on her birthday, well," he sighed. "She's really something, isn't she?"

"She sure is," I said, feeling an immediate and irrepressible urge to make like a Mack truck right out of there. I rose suddenly to my feet, nearly spilling my glass of wine.

Ben looked at me in confusion. "Are you leaving?"

"Yes, you know, motherhood," I said, forcing an awkward laugh. "I'm sure my babysitter wants to get home." I beelined for the coat rack.

Ben hurried after me. "Heidi, wait. Don't you have anything to say about what I asked you? About Annie?" He planted himself in front of the door to bar my exit.

I averted my gaze. "You know, Ben, you're an adult. You should do what you want. And as far as Annie's response, well, I guess you'll just have to ask her yourself." I turned the doorknob and pulled, letting in a gust of December air. "As you said, we are no longer children. We sure shouldn't act like it." I gave a weak smile and escaped to my car. Turning the key, I cranked the shift into reverse and sped the few blocks to my house.

My car jolted to a stop in our driveway. I cut the lights. Sitting in the dark, my forehead on the steering wheel, I felt the warmth of embarrassment fill my cheeks.

Tahiti, for crying out loud.

And worse, he wanted to ask out my best friend.

Childish behavior indeed. I angrily wiped away hot tears of shame before unloading the trunk and ascending our porch steps, not at all eager to face my all-grown-up life.

ℰ ⅁ ℰ

You know what they say about desperate times.

After Lauren's mom came to pick her up and I'd brushed and flossed, I flopped down on our bed. For a moment I just sat, wondering how I'd come to feel so out of control of the life I'd built for myself.

Peering through the open closet door, I glimpsed a neatly stacked pile of Jake's T-shirts, color coordinated and alphabetized. I walked over to the stack, picked out a worn light blue one that read "Sal's Pizza — Family Run and Taste Bud Friendly Since 1957." Jake and I had eaten at Sal's on our first date during college. I could still taste their Canadian bacon and pineapple when I thought of it years later. I stood in the closet, holding Jake's shirt to my nose, inhaling his scent. I pulled it over my head and returned to bed.

The minutes ticked by as I stared into the dark, waiting for a visit from sleep. Six thirty would come bright and early, and I needed to be ready to go full throttle.

Visualizing a herd of frolicking sheep did nothing.

Lamaze breathing proved just as ineffectual postpartum as it had in the delivery room.

In frustration, I flicked on my bedside lamp and huffed. Images of Ben and Annie, Jake and Jana, Nora and Rina drifted through my head. Not one of them was smiling. Never had I felt so completely responsible for failure on so many fronts.

Ben had rejected me, though I'm not sure he'd even known about my Tahiti agenda.

Jake felt far, far away and could, for all I knew, be on a plane somewhere right now to a snow-covered chalet owned by the Van Fleet family.

I'd made Annie feel like a tool for looking out for her best friend's sanity.

Nora loved me, but only because I gave her Cheerios. Anyway, she probably liked Lauren more.

Eyes closed, I waited impatiently for the relief of slumber.

I was just about to head to the medicine chest and dig around for some kind of sleeping narcotic when I saw Jake's Bible on his nightstand. I considered it with a wary eye, weighing whether or not the narcotic would be more efficient. Jake had marked a page in the middle somewhere. A skinny ribbon stuck out where he'd been reading. I opened up to a page with "Matthew" written at the top. Jake had underlined a verse in red, smack in the middle of the page. I imagined him with a straight edge, tongue out as he concentrated on drawing perfectly parallel lines. I looked to see what had struck him. Jesus was talking:

"Come to me. Get away with me and you'll recover your life. I'll show you how to take a real rest. . . . Keep company with me and you'll learn to live freely and lightly."

A lump rose in my throat. Live freely and lightly. If I had to offer some adverbs to describe my recent heart activity, I definitely would not have chosen "freely" or "lightly." In fact, I could feel my frantic heart treading water in the middle of the ocean, my only tool a broken compass.

I closed my eyes. I felt the words choke in my chest as I said aloud, "God, help me fix my mess."

I didn't know if that even counted as a prayer; I certainly wouldn't be volunteering to say any showstoppers for Moms' Group anytime soon. But after a minute the room slowed on its axis and my head cleared enough for me to switch off the light and lie down again. I rolled onto my side, getting a whiff of Jake's clean, familiar smell just before my eyes shut for good. I dreamed all night about lazy drifting on an endless turquoise ocean.

chapter/eighteen

Back at school on Monday, I forced myself to go through the motions, hovering around the perimeter of activity without ever engaging. The hallways vibrated with anticipation of winter break, which began after school Friday. Classrooms dripped with holiday decorations, most teachers submitting to the politically correct snowflakes and snowmen but the renegades among us bringing in contraband Christmas trees.

Micah and Darren stopped by my desk on their way out of class. "Are you going to Holly Daze, Mrs. Elliott?" Micah asked, looking ridiculous in a furry Santa hat.

During my drive through downtown that morning, I'd noticed the streets were already cloaked in acres of tinsel and lights in anticipation of Saturday's festival.

"*Sí, claro*," I answered, erasing the board before my next class. "I'll be there with silver bells on."

Too young for both the cliché and the song, the boys merely nodded. Darren said, "Sweet. Look for me in my grandpa's Studebaker. He's letting me drive it this year." He grinned.

I feared for the safety of parade goers. "You better throw me some candy," I said, wiping the chalk off my hands. "I'll pretend it's for Nora, but as long as she's still toothless, all loot goes to *mamá*."

Darren laughed as he left the room, saying over his bulky defensive-end shoulder, "*Muy* sly, *Señora*."

I turned to Micah. "I liked the poem."

Micah grunted, but looked pleased. "It wasn't a poem. It was song lyrics. For me and my band."

"A band?" I said, trying to sound hip. "Nice. Where's your next gig?"

He smirked. "Our next gig is our biggest so far. On the courthouse stage at Holly Daze. Be there," he said, tossing his hair out of his face to get a line of sight on the door.

"Wouldn't miss it," I said, watching him go.

To be frank, forcing this cavalier attitude was wearing me out. Survival skills kicked in at school, where I put on my Pollyanna face and played the part of Happily Fulfilled Teacher. Inside, however, I was limping around a high pile of hurts, not sure where to start picking up the debris.

At the top of the list, I felt embarrassed about my struggling marriage and the canyon of distance I'd helped create. After so many months of neglect, I was fearful of what would happen if I confronted our marital landmine. What if Jake didn't love me anymore? What if he was planning a trip to the Alps and had already checked into lawyer fees?

What if I was too late?

Shudder Number Two came when I pictured the scene at Ben's house on Sunday. It was one thing to be cast aside by a former ex, but to be shunned for one's best friend was an extra twist to the knife. Never mind that I was supposed to be unavailable and uninterested. The mere proximity of rejection reminded me of yet another area of inadequacy and shed unforgiving light on the holes in my marriage.

Annie and I had spoken since my outburst over tea, but we were still tiptoeing in our conversations. We so seldom felt alienated from each other that we didn't really know how to find our way back to "normal." I hadn't told her about my conversation with Ben, figuring she'd tell me if he called. And if she didn't, well, there was something to be said for the blissfully ignorant.

Topping off my woes, Nora was back at Rina's during the day, and I hated it. At least one of us cried at drop-off and/or pick-up. Rina merely looked on in carefully suppressed horror, her impenetrable smile twitching with discomfort. Babies, parents, subordinates—people just didn't cry in front of Rina.

In short, I was losing on all fronts.

So it was with heavy heart that I bundled Nora up for her first Holly Daze parade on Saturday. Jake busied himself loading the car with a Thermos of apple cider, snacks for Nora, and down blankets to keep out the chill of bleacher seats.

"Why, I ask you, do we celebrate an outdoor winter festival in Minnesota?" I muttered to Nora as I snapped her into her snowsuit. Only her eyes were exposed when I'd finished. "Why don't we have, say, a blueberry pie festival in the summer, or a daffodil festival in the spring? Pumpkin festival in the fall?" I stuffed the pockets of my coat with Kleenex to combat the familial runny nose. "Does it not bear consideration that Springdale is not favorably situated with regard to the equator?"

"Who's the Scrooge in here, bug?" Jake asked Nora as he lifted her pink Michelin frame.

"Meeeshmee," Nora sang, her voice muffled by layers of fabric.

Straightening up, I moved stiffly in a turtleneck, flannel shirt, sweater, jeans, ski pants, and thermal underwear. I began buttoning my final layer, my "only if it's well below zero *or* Holly Daze" coat, and Jake reached over to help. I watched his hands as he buttoned me up, riveted with his sudden tenderness.

He touched my nose with his index finger, lifted my chin. "It'll be good to spend some time as a family, right, Scrooge?" He attempted a sheepish smile, a flicker of uncertainty in his eyes.

"Absolutely," I said, looking away.

Jake lugged Nora to the car, which was warming in the driveway. I looked up to the sky. Mary Jo Willard and her festival minions would be pleased. The day was clear and nearly cloudless. The sun shone with as much winter strength as it could muster, and though nothing was melting under its rays, the extra light would boost people's spirits. High spirits translated into more festival participants, more fruitcakes sold, and more cameras from local news channels. The Holly Daze diehards went in freezing rain and blizzards, but good weather was a plus for the weanies among us.

I locked the front door behind me, walked to the car, and crawled in the passenger seat. Nora blew raspberries in the back as we crawled through traffic, everyone eager to get a parking spot near the center of town.

After nabbing a space near Maurizio's, we threaded our way through the throng of revelers. Jake led our charge, opening a brief path for me and Nora. The sidewalks had been cleared of snow and ice for the festival. Melting salts crunched under the stroller wheels. Hearing nothing from within, I peeked in the canopy window. Nora's long eyelashes drooped, already responding to the swaying lullaby of the stroller.

We passed the downtown shops and their decorated window displays. Mulligan Brothers' Hardware had removed their usual toolboxes and stepladders and replaced them with a train set. A crowd of kids stood gawking as it wound its circular track. Farther down, Nettie's Knit-N-Stitch had glued glittered pinecones into an outline of a reindeer. Not so many gawkers at that one. My favorite window was at Parker Books, where hundreds of books, spine side out, stacked together to form a multicolored literary Christmas tree.

As we walked, Jake and I took turns greeting clients and school folk, respectively, occasionally stopping long enough for friendly festival banter.

"Have you seen the tinsel forest this year? Just *breathtaking*."

"Not yet, Mrs. Schwimmer, but we'll make sure to take a look."

"Hello, David, Mr. and Mrs. Martinez. Where did you find that hot chocolate?"

"Booth just down the way, Mrs. Elliott. Mike and Melissa Hargrove's place."

"Why, is this little Nora? She's growing like a weed!"

"Lucky for her, Mrs. Bertoli, she looks like her mother."

"Now, Jake, don't you start. . . ."

For once, I found mindless blather comforting. What if people wanted honest answers to their questions? Could you imagine?

"Why, Heidi, you look so drawn and tired. Is anything the matter?"

"Actually, Mrs. Woods, I'm feeling the burden of balancing work, family, and personal relationships and failing miserably at all three. My husband here—say hello, Jake—could be boinking a Swedish love princess, and my ex-boyfriend, who should not even exist on my emotional radar, recently dumped me for my best friend, but not before I had considered wrecking my family to be with him. I'm not sure how I'm doing as a mom, though Nora has avoided incarceration up to this point. Say, can I try your funnel cake?"

Much safer to say the same things in every stupid conversation without ever really hearing each other.

After some serious stroller Olympics, we obtained a space on the bleachers where Jake and I could share a seat just the right size for the mayor of Munchkinland. We parked Nora on the walkway beside us. Jake and I, forced to be close, got acclimated to our view.

The festival was in full swing. The parade route was crowded with people searching for empty seats. Three elementary school boys ran by, pelting a fourth with snowballs. A man carried his daughter on his shoulders, her pixie face glowing with the cold and the promise of cotton candy. In front of us sat an older couple, huddled together under a patchwork quilt, laughing together at the candy-caned stickiness of a child's face.

Jake draped his arm across my shoulders and pulled me to him. "Happy Holly Daze, Heidi," he said into my ear, giving me a peck on one of my red cheeks.

"You, too," I said, turning into him. I smelled his aftershave, felt his whiskers on my lips.

I'd missed him.

I nuzzled my face into his neck, feeling its warmth thaw my frozen nose. His Adam's apple moved abruptly when he shouted across the packed street.

"Hello there!"

His waving arm jarred me upright. I looked to see the recipient of his summons. With the shimmer of ten carats in an all-white ski outfit, Jana Van Fleet spotted us from her perch in the parade's only sky box. Ms. Van Fleet and her perky bosom returned Jake's salute and started down the steps and toward the cheap seats.

"Wow," I said, not even trying to veil my disgust. If I hadn't known better, I'd have thought the woman was campaigning for Snow Princess, which traditionally was limited to girls between the ages of four and six. White coat, white skin-tight pants exposing the fruits of all those hours in the gym, toffee-colored snow boots trimmed with white fur.

If I'd tried something like that, the effect would have been something like a chinchilla on crack.

On Jana, it was stunning.

"Jake, how *are* you?" Jana gushed, leaning forward to offer a rosy cheek sprinkled with glitter. With the lips he'd just used on me, Jake kissed Jana and she him. I hoped she'd try that with me so I could give her a nice, swift kick in the—

"Jana, you remember my wife and daughter." Jake peered into the foggy stroller window at our sleeping offspring.

"Of course, of course. It's good to see you again, Haley," Jana said, gracing me with a Miss America smile.

"It's Heidi," I said, straight-faced.

Jana didn't hear my correction, as she was poised over the stroller like a kitten waiting to pounce. She made a big show of sighing at Nora's beauty, calling her an angel, complimenting Jake on his gene pool.

"Well," I said loudly, "I think I'll go get some hot chocolate. Anyone else want anything?" Extra knives for my back? Quick-sign divorce papers from Office Depot?

"Sure," Jake said, reaching for his wallet. "Hot chocolate with whipped cream, please."

I looked at Jana. "No thank you, Hannah." She patted her flat stomach. "Must watch all those calories during the holiday season." She laughed and Jake joined in appreciatively.

I wanted to puke.

Striding toward the nearest hot chocolate stand, I heard the school marching band coming around the first corner of the parade route. I hurried down the sidewalk, willing my heart to rebound from its sunken state. Walking against the flow of the band, I glimpsed many of my students passing in a sea of blue and gold. Lindsay Patterson concentrated furiously on her trombone. Shanita Morrow flashed me a grin from her post at the bass drum. Mr. Weinhöfen looked like he was going to collapse keeping time alongside the clarinets.

I plunked down enough money for two hot chocolates and stood facing the parade and sipping my drink. Jessica Collins caught my eye from atop the Holly Queen's float and waved as regally as her furry gloves and hat would allow. A few slots later, Darren Smits chucked a huge handful of candy over the crowd at me, shouting, "Give a couple to Nora, okay?"

I raised my Styrofoam cup to him, and to Ana López, who sat next to him in the passenger seat of the green Studebaker. Rocks filled my chest watching them, remembering vividly the vulnerability of first love.

I felt ancient.

A group of Shriners in tasseled hats followed Darren and Ana, waving miniature American flags and tossing orange circus peanuts. I stayed and sipped through six Santas, the baton twirling club, the Ladies' Auxiliary's purple and red tractor, and the Class of 1984's float. This year's theme was "Winter Paradise" and featured aging graduates in beach gear, the cold effectively numbed by persistent alcohol consumption and blaring Jimmy Buffett.

My hot chocolate half-gone, I started back to our bleacher seats. With any holiday luck, Jana Van Vomit would be gone by now and I'd be able to spend the rest of the parade with Jake, simmering in self-pity.

Half a block away, I got stuck behind a gaggle of middle school girls engaged in hyperactive chatter about someone named Tucker. Not one of them had listened to their mothers and worn hats. They'd shellacked their collective hairdo so fiercely into place, not even a blizzard would have moved one set of bangs. My patience dwindled as they moved on to another boy named Harrison. I said as sweetly as I could muster, "Excuse me, girls." After repeating my request for the third time, the sea parted reluctantly, and I squeezed my way through.

Intent on not spilling Jake's lukewarm chocolate, it took me a moment to focus on who stood before me. Leaning against the brick wall of Sally's Beauty Nook was Annie.

I stopped dead in my tracks.

Facing her and leaning in close to talk was Ben. Even from fifty feet away, I could see Annie's eyes sparkle with laughter. With feigned indignation, she pushed him playfully, and he grabbed her hand and held it. She looked down, her smile subdued, expectant.

I shivered myself into action, ducking my head and passing Annie and Ben unnoticed. My nose marked my quick progress past the waffle cones, hot dogs, and caramel corn. Approaching our bleacher, I saw Jana had wedged herself into my mini-seat and was absorbed with her snow bunny theatrics.

I pushed my way toward them until I faced them squarely. "Jake," I said, engulfed in a wave of sadness.

He looked up expectantly, Jana still twittering about something he'd said.

I shoved the cup into his hand, spilling half the whipped cream on his trousers, turned, and walked away.

"Heidi, where are you going?"

I heard Jake calling after me, but I just kept trucking.

I walked at least twenty minutes without breaking stride, not even stopping to spy on Dr. Willard and Stillwell, who were huddled in the hardware store alley, whispering furiously. I elbowed my way through a Santa convention, half of them already shedding their fake beards in order to save them from corn dog grease. Near the courthouse I heard the strains of angry garage band music. Micah and three others in black stood strumming, drumming, and wailing under a banner that read "Traumatic Static." He nodded at me as I passed, hammering relentlessly on a bass guitar.

Ten blocks along, I realized I had no keys to the car and was still at least three miles from home. My nose had lost all feeling in the cold. The moisture in my eyelashes was freezing into little clumps. I'd made it as far as Westridge Shopping Mall when a car pulled up beside me.

Determined not to look in case it was Jake, I trudged on, eyes fixed on the horizon. I heard the passenger side window being lowered.

"Heidi?" Willow leaned over the seat to open the door. "Get in, you nut. What are you doing out here?"

I stopped, looked long at her concerned face.

Without protest, my legs carried me to her beat-up Volkswagen, stepped in, and folded in front of me as I shut the door. I stared straight ahead, saying nothing.

"Put on your seat belt," Willow instructed gently.

I obeyed.

She put the car in gear and we started toward what I hoped would be a warm place.

chapter/nineteen

Willow's gallery was a block off Main in what used to be a church. The original approach to the building remained, weathered limestone steps leading to a Gothic arch. After passing through two mammoth carved doors, however, resemblance to what had been St. Peter's Episcopal dropped off sharply.

Willow flipped the light switch, breaking into the gray dusk of winter. The space inside was light and airy, belying the church's heavy outer façade. White walls grew into a vaulted ceiling, interrupted three quarters of the way up by massive windows trimmed in stained glass. The stone floor, cleared of St. Peter's pews, supported five or six groupings of artwork by local artists. I followed Willow through the middle of the sanctuary, collections of pottery, glass, and oil paintings flanking each side.

We walked up a narrow staircase and down a hallway to reach what had been the choir loft in days of old. During non–Holly Daze time, the Loft was open for light lunch and coffee, but today it was deserted. Ten or so small tables held stem vases of single poinsettia blooms. Several of the tables sat right up against the loft railing and looked out onto the sanctuary/gallery.

Willow steered me toward one of the railing tables, and I slumped in my chair, waiting as she made coffee behind the mosaic-tiled counter at the back. Her auburn hair was unusually light, backlit by a kaleidoscopic stained glass window on the back wall. She worked efficiently, as if well versed in picking up the pieces for catatonic shock victims out strolling in subzero weather.

I cupped the steaming mug she offered with both hands, adding all the sugar and cream I could stomach. She sat opposite me, sipping, waiting for color to creep back into my cheeks.

After a long, long while, the caffeine and Willow's unwavering patience coaxed me out of my silence. I began, in quiet, careful words, to tell Willow what had led up to abandoning my family on the curb of a holiday parade. Soon the words rushed out of me, eager to be heard, jumping to leave the cage where I'd kept them for months. I started with Jake, moved on to Annie and Ben, recycled Jake, touched on Nora and work, threw in some choice words on Jana Van Fleet, then fell silent, spent. My coffee cup was empty. Willow got up to refill it.

When she returned, I took a long swig, not even caring that it scalded off 75 percent of my taste buds. I pulled the cup away from my mouth, staring into the steam as I swirled the coffee into a lazy whirlpool.

Willow reached out to still the mug, and when I set it down, she covered my hands with hers. Looking up, I was surprised to see tears covering her freckled cheeks.

"Don't worry," she said, tears falling freely. "I cry about insurance commercials." She blew her nose. "You just remind me of myself at your age, though I don't think you smoke pot."

True enough. "Why? Did you have a hard time balancing work and family, too?"

"Oh, no," she said. "I was sleeping with a different man every week in a commune in northern California."

Good grief, I thought. Do I really want to hear this?

"I said I was there to escape the war-loving, peace-hating world, smoke weed, and free myself from the constraints of the status quo. But I was really there to thumb my nose at my parents and anyone else who'd tried to control me."

"Is that where you met your husband?"

She nodded, smiling to herself. "He loved me from the start, he always said. It took me a while to come around, though. I thought he was bizarre."

"Bizarre even to a hashish-smoking hippy?"

She laughed. "Sure. Just on the other end of the spectrum. He was always smiling but never high. Really kind, old-school polite. And he carried this leather Bible around with him all the time. Like an evangelist in love beads. I thought he was nuts." She shook her head. "I wasn't touching Jesus Boy with a ten-foot pole."

"So what changed your mind?"

"Even with the Jesus talk, Michael was spicy enough to keep me interested. I'd met my match." She smiled. "And I'd tried everything else. Michael knew about something, rather Someone, who could fill the void."

I braced myself for the God pitch.

"Jesus ended up being even more stubborn than I am." She got up to rinse our cups. "But you'll find that out on your own, if you're interested. God doesn't need me to sell Him to you like a used car."

I relaxed. I seemed to be clear of the Bible-beating risk zone. Just to be sure, I changed the subject. "Willow, what do I do about my marriage?"

"Oh, honey, my advice isn't only free, it's usually worthless. You'll have to wade through that just the two of you. But," she said, eyes bright and trained on mine, "if I were you, I'd fight. It'll get uglier before it gets better, but I'd put up my dukes and fight for my marriage."

I swallowed. "What if it's too late?"

"Too late is when you're dead. Trust me. You and Jake love each other, but you've gotten lazy about it. My guess is the Swedish chick is only symptomatic." She shook her head. "It's usually not about the boobs."

We pulled on our coats and started down the stairs of the Loft, Willow extinguishing the lights as we went. When we reached the big front doors, she put a hand on my arm to stop me. She disappeared behind an old bookkeeping desk near the entrance and returned with a book in her hand.

"Here," she said. She held out a leather-bound Bible, its cover worn, the gold-leafed pages dulled from use. The corners of her mouth upturned in a small smile. "This was the obnoxious thing that prevented me from dating my husband for the first two years I knew him."

I shook my head. "I can't take this."

Willow nodded. "Yes, you can. I have my own, you know. And Michael would click his little Jesus freak heels to know it was getting passed on to a dear friend." She watched me, her eyes bright with kindness.

I took the book in my hands, felt the smooth cover, let the thin pages run front to back. "Thanks," I said. "I don't really know what to do with it," I admitted.

Willow laughed, pushed open the carved door. "Crack it open and take a look when you get the gumption. I've found it usually does more to me than I do to it."

I followed her outside, tucking the Bible in an inside pocket of my parka. We stood in the cold, letting our eyes adjust to the darkness that was falling fast.

"Can I give you a ride?" she asked.

I nodded and let her drive me to a hundred-year-old house on Winwood Lane.

℮ ℈ ℮

All was quiet when I unlocked the front door and stepped inside. Through the baby monitor I could hear Jake putting Nora down for a late nap. I sat on the couch in the living room, still in my coat.

The door to the nursery opened and closed quietly. Jake appeared and saw me sitting in the fading light of afternoon. "Hi."

"Hi."

He walked to an armchair and sat. "Where were you?"

"I needed to take a walk."

He nodded slowly. "Do you think you could have called?"

My blood pressure started to rise. "Do you think you could have refrained from publicly humiliating your wife?"

Jake opened both his hands in exasperation. "Heidi, if you're talking about Jana—"

"Well, this is progress. At least you're acknowledging I might have a problem with you sitting with a floozy in full view of the whole town." I stood up and unzipped my parka.

"Jana is a client. A really important one. Did you expect me to ignore her, for Pete's sake?"

"I don't know, Jake," I said from the closet as I hung up my coat and took off my scarf. "You're the Christian around here. What would Jesus stinkin' do?" I stepped out of the closet and saw his ashen face. "Seriously," I continued. "I've gone to your church group. I've even struck up a friendship with a former peacenik. And where has it gotten us, Jake? You're on the brink of sleeping with a Swedish beer commercial—if you haven't already—and I'm the emptiest I've ever felt." I stopped, my words forming a lump in my throat.

Jake looked away. "Heidi," he said, "I'm sorry."

I shook my head, felt hot tears on my cheeks. "I think you should leave."

He sat motionless, breathless. Then he stood up. And left.

℮ ℈ ℮

So there I sat, still in my long underwear and ski pants and starting to sweat. I cried like a baby. It was an ugly cry, one that made me gasp, hiccup, and snort up reams of sinus debris.

First it was an angry cry. My mind scrolled through images of Jake with Jana, my husband's lack of courage, lack of emotional fidelity, failure to acknowledge how lucky he was to have married up. Then I transitioned to a pity-party cry. I reviewed all the ways in which I'd been wronged, the pathetic loser I'd become, the slime pit I'd made of my life. This was also the chocolate peanut butter cup ice cream stage. I rolled right through a pint and went back for frozen waffles for dessert.

Full of empty calories and drained of tears, I sat staring. I wanted Nora to wake up, to give me some distraction from my disaster. But she was silent, the poor thing tuckered out from Holly Daze and temporary maternal abandonment.

That thought threw me into my last crying jag, this one of full-blown remorse. Talk about the pot calling the kettle black: I'd just chewed out my husband for dabbling where I'd already dabbled. Visions of Ben and his candlelit living room brought fresh waves of shame and humiliation. My shoulders shook with sobs. After a moment, I heard myself repeating, "Help. Please help."

I stopped long enough to collect myself and walk to the hall closet. I fumbled for the light switch and pulled on the sleeve of my parka. I opened the coat enough to yank Michael's Bible from the inside pocket. Carrying it back to the couch, I opened it and blinked through my swollen lids. This is what I saw:

> *"Are you tired? Worn out? Burned out on religion? Come to me. Get away with me and you'll recover your life. I'll show you how to take a rest. Walk with me and work with me—watch how I do it. Learn the unforced rhythms of grace. I won't lay anything heavy or ill-fitting on you. Keep company with me and you'll learn to live freely and lightly."*

I didn't know whether to feel totally creeped out or amazed. I'd read the Bible outside of a pew maybe three times in my twenty-nine years, but two of those three had involved this "freely and lightly" thing.

"All right," I prayed aloud, my face caked with salt from my weeping. "I'm opening the door a crack. I guess You can come in."

And wouldn't you know it, He did.

❧ ❧ ❧

Jake and I treated each other cautiously the next morning, still stinging from yesterday's blowup. The night before he'd taken in a late movie and gone straight to bed. Today, when he left for work, I called Willow to see if she'd be willing to have Nora for a slumber party.

"You'd better believe it," she said without hesitating. "Estrogen has been outnumbered by testosterone for so many years in this house, it's about time a girl came to visit."

"Thanks," I said. "It'll be much easier to confront a crumbling marriage without having to change diapers."

"Are you nervous?" she asked.

"Very."

"I'll pray about it."

"When I can come up for air, I want to talk with you about that. There's something I . . ."

She waited, but when I fell silent, she said, "Absolutely. I'm ready to talk when you are. I'll see you and Nora in an hour."

That afternoon I took Nora's playpen with me even though Willow had said she could use the twins' old crib. It was hidden in her attic somewhere, she said, but she was sure she could figure it out and put it together. Knowing well that at least sixty people died each year due to complications arising during crib assemblage, I declined and supplied our Pack 'N Play.

An hour later, I stood waiting by the front door, candles lit, pizza ordered, chocolate lava cakes ready for the oven. I marked items off my list, while Mexico's entire migration of Monarch butterflies fluttered in my stomach. I glimpsed our empty driveway for the hundredth time.

Finally, headlights swept our darkened dining room, and I saw Jake unfold from his pickup. I struck what I hoped was a relaxed pose on the couch. He shoved open the front door, arms full of papers and mail. Confusion swept over his face at the greeting of quiet calm instead of our normal suppertime trapeze act.

"Heidi?" he called before letting his eyes rest on me. I was wearing something that will need to remain undisclosed here. Just know it was Jake's gift from our last pre-pregs Valentine's Day, and I fit into it again. Quite well, in fact.

He smiled shyly. "So the candles don't mean I should call an electrician?"

I slid my arms around his neck and whispered in his ear, "Hi, honey. I'm home."

℮ ♋ ℮

Man, did we have fun that night. And I don't just mean with *that*, though *that* was awfully good, too. It was an evening unencumbered by responsibilities: no baby monitors crackling, no dishes to wash or lunches to pack, no looming early

morning beckoning us to sleep. Just the two of us, a candlelit
house, and a large Hawaiian combo from Sal's.

I laid the ground rules before we had one bite of pizza.
First, we would not call Willow unless one of us had punc-
tured a lung or major artery. Second, we would not discuss
Nora, parenting strategies, or even her undeniable brilliance.
Finally, we would kiss like honeymooners every hour on the
hour, unless the previous hour's kissing ran into the next.

Jake raised not one objection.

We talked as we hadn't for months, maybe years. I gathered
my courage and told Jake everything, and I mean everything.

"I thought he was trying to seduce me," I said about the
photo shoots with Ben.

"Did you want him to?" Jake asked, his eyes locked with
mine.

It took everything in me, but I nodded. "I'm so sorry, Jake.
I hate talking about this, but we have to."

"So why didn't it happen?"

"Because Ben wasn't even interested. And because Nora
peed and pooped all over his shirt."

Jake smiled to himself. "That's my girl."

"I love you, Jake. I'm sorry my heart wandered, even if no
one else knew."

He nodded, still processing. Then he looked up. "My
turn."

"Okay, but it's nine. Time to kiss."

We did.

"Are you trying to distract me from the business at hand?"
he said, face close to mine.

"Maybe," I said.

He pulled away, held my shoulders and my gaze. "Heidi, I need to ask for your forgiveness."

My heart sank. "Jana?"

"Yes, Jana, but it's not what you think."

"Start talking."

Jake told me how he'd kept the Van Fleet project to himself, even when he knew Rob should take over. He said he'd looked for extra opportunities to have meetings with Jana, that even though they'd never ended up touching each other, he was wrong to even entertain the possibility. Then he told me a slew of hilarious stories involving the Swedish Princess of Neuroses. Turns out Jana had great legs but wasn't exactly working with a full deck, no matter what her doctored-up ACT score read.

He shook his head. "My behavior is even more disgusting because I should know better."

"You mean the Christian thing?"

"Yes," he said. "I even kept reading my Bible through the whole experience. I justified it all by telling myself I deserved to feel interesting again since my wife was too distant to notice anymore."

Gulp. "I think you're interesting," I protested.

Jake raised his eyebrow. "You think I'm predictable."

I hedged. "What's wrong with predictable? Predictability is an admirable trait."

"In dogs. Weather patterns. Mailmen."

"I like all those things."

He shook his head. "I bored you."

"Untrue."

"Were you not shocked when I ordered Gorgonzola gnocchi that night at Maurizio's?"

"But, see? You proved me dead wrong. Utterly unpredictably wrong. You ate the whole thing!"

Jake looked sheepish. "Out of spite. I hated it."

I cleared my throat and cocked an eyebrow.

"Heidi," he said, holding my face in his hands, "I am wild about you. No one amazes me like you do. No one makes me laugh like you do. No one comes close." His voice broke. "I'm so sorry I even messed with that."

"Do you forgive me?" I said, my face against his wet cheek.

"Yes. Me?"

"Yes." I tightened my grip around his neck. "But if you ever so much as look at a Swedish woman again, I'll kill you."

"And may all famous photographers be doomed to lives of loneliness and sterility."

"Isn't that a bit harsh?" I asked, pushing him onto his back.

His eyes widened. "That was my censored version."

I giggled as he pulled me down for a kiss.

epilogue

It's been four months now since my crumbling-marriage talk with Jake and my "I give up" talk with God. I have this amazing light feeling in my chest, and it's not just because I've stopped nursing. It feels like there's a big, fluffy pillow that's moved in around my heart, cradling and catching it before it falls and smashes into a billion pieces. Willow calls it grace.

Not to say, of course, that life around here is all wine and roses. I still languish through weeks, months sometimes, when I try to take over, thanking God for His cooperation but telling Him to move over 'cause I'm driving. Remembering I'm not in charge of the universe does not seem to come naturally to me, but Molly Langdon says that's normal.

I've never found it productive to argue with Molly Langdon.

Annie and I are pretty much back to our usual selves. It took a while, especially considering she's dating Ben. That gets a little sticky, I must say. But it has become easier to wish her the best, even if it means she's the one going to Tahiti. She and Ben seem to get along famously, though Ben's artistic temperament (read: Van-Gogh-I'm-about-to-cut-off-someone's-ear-and-stick-it-in-the-mail moodiness) drives her nuts. For his part, Ben sleeps in and is morally opposed to running long distances unless being pursued by terrorists, so both parties will have to give. Can't see any double dates in our future, but at least Jake has stopped breaking out into hives at the mention of Ben's name.

Besides, Tahiti has lost its appeal. Jake and I have a standing appointment with each other every Thursday evening while Lauren babysits. Ground rules still apply, so we're talking, even when I don't feel like it. It's good to find your husband again and like him even better the second time around.

This whole thing about not needing to do and be everything has given me new courage to break wide open my definition of myself. For one, stepping off the tightrope on which I've wobbled this year doesn't seem quite so ludicrous. In fact, I've decided to ditch the entire balancing act and stay at home with Nora.

Mind you, this is on a trial basis. Dr. Willard granted me a one-year unpaid sabbatical, offering to hold my job for me should I decide being a "professional mommy" wasn't for me. In light of continuing our professional relationship, I decided not to discuss what appears to be his part in a lecherous affair. I, for one, have learned a valuable lesson on fidelity and wasted moments. But I am only a teacher of Spanish, not of life lessons to men in polyester suits. Though I ache for Ms. Stillwell and hope she finds her way to a less tortured state—like maybe Arizona—I realize I cannot do everything. I've been practicing that line: "I cannot do everything. I cannot do everything." Am I convincing yet?

Regarding becoming a stay-at-home mom, I have my reservations. A maternity leave is one thing, but when I think of the days stretching in front of me, with Nora's high school graduation the only goal, I get nervous. What if it's mind-numbing? What if I can't handle the absence of adult interaction? What if I start dressing like a slob whose only joy in life is daytime television? What if Nora gets sick of me? What if she becomes a social misfit with an unhealthy attachment to her mother?

These questions dart around my mind in dangerous acrobatic swirls, particularly in the moments right before sleep. My eyes snap open, disturbed by visions of a frumpy me in sweats, schlepping around the mall, pushing a triple-wide stroller with three screaming kids.

I shudder.

When I remember, though, I give myself a quick talk down from the rafters and sneak a peek at Michael's Bible. There's a section at the back that tells you where to look when you're feeling stressed, confused, alone, hormonal, and so forth. And it gives page numbers, which are helpful for those of us who didn't know until last week that Exodus wasn't just a Bob Marley song. Right now I'm reading the Psalms. Some of the passages are pure poetry, just beautiful. Others are on the angry side and focus on God smiting people you dislike. I could have used a few of those during the Van Fleet experience.

Right now Nora and I are in the park, waiting for Jake to show up for an after-work play date. I've laid a blanket on a patch of Technicolor green that heralds the official arrival of spring. A warm breeze tickles Nora's peach fuzz hair; she gasps and grins, soaking in the after-winter world.

Out of the corner of my eye, I spot someone checking us out. I look up to see Micah, the gnome artist. Still in black but with extra piercings, he stands several feet away, trying to look nonchalant while fiddling with a beat-up skateboard.

"Hi, Micah," I say, smiling in his direction.

"Well, if it isn't my favorite teacher of *español*," he drawls, one side of his mouth creeping toward a smile before he remembers to keep up the coolness quotient. "Is this the kid?" He nods his head at Nora.

"She's the one," I say, smooshing her nose with a fresh Kleenex.

Micah plops down next to Nora and allows her hand to curl around his index finger. For a moment, I glimpse the face his mother probably remembers from before junior high, one open enough to make a child laugh. If I squint the right way, Micah's a cutie under those bangs and eyebrow rings.

"I registered for Spanish III for this fall," he says, sticking out his tongue at my daughter. People in our house don't have tongue piercings, so Nora's eyes bug out of her head in awe.

"That's awesome," I say. "I'm sorry I won't be there to confiscate your spitball weaponry. Or become your band's oldest groupie."

Micah looks up at me. "Aren't you coming back?"

I shake my head. "I'm taking a break for a while. Gonna spend some serious time with Nora before she's old enough to score some rad half axles on your board there."

Micah rolls his eyes at my antiquated lingo.

"People don't say 'rad' anymore, do they?" I ask, suppressing a smile.

Micah shakes his head. He pulls himself to his feet and flips up one end of his skateboard with a grungy sneaker. "I hope the new teacher's not a freak," he says by way of good-bye.

Then, over his shoulder, he says, "Kid's pretty cute. I can see why you'd want to be around for her."

I smile at his back as he skates away, putting his life and others in peril by navigating through hair, around small metal objects attached to his face, and above the dragging hems of huge jeans. And people say teenagers can't multitask.

I throw Nora in the air a few times and carry her to the playground. She clings to the baby swing while I Boogey Man her feet on the downward swoops. She's giggling like a hyena. Over her wild arcs I see Jake cresting the hill, hands in his pockets and a grin on his face.

"Daddy's coming, peanut," I say, drinking in the beauty of their twin smiles in a single line of sight.

Jake lifts me off the ground to kiss me, and Nora squeals at her parents, the celebrities. I close my eyes and fill my lungs with clean April air. It's been nearly a year since the steak and stitches, and I'm no longer afraid to open *National Geographic*.

A little grace goes a long way.

etc.

bonus content includes:

- ▸ Reader's Guide

- ▸ Micah's Songbook

- ▸ Willow's Pasta of Love

- ▸ Sneak Preview of Sequel to *Balancing Act*

- ▸ Author's Note: Living Proof

- ▸ About the Author

reader's guide

Heidi's Questions

1. Women living in the United States in the twenty-first century are endowed with greater freedom than ever before. In light of this fact, does that mean I'm a whining pansy, unable to balance a charmed life?

2. I once read an article in *Redbook* that pointed out the many advantages of having a little affair in order to spice up a boring marriage. How does this strike you? Was any part of you secretly hoping Jake or I would go from dabbling to taking the plunge? What, if anything, is dangerous about dabbling?

3. I found my work environment to be less than supportive of my dual role as a professional and a mother. Did this resonate with your own experience or the experience of someone you know? What is your idea of a perfectly balanced work/home situation?

Jake's Questions

1. If you had to choose between a painter and a photographer, who would you choose? Keep in mind no photographer even uses a darkroom anymore.

2. When our daughter, Nora, came along, our sex life took a turn for the nonexistent. Do you think it's okay to mention that in a Christian novel? Is there a chance Kimberly Stuart will be canned before her next book goes to press?

3. If you aren't afraid of a little book club honesty, discuss if/how couples with small children can stoke the fires of love, even amid pacifiers and sleepless nights.

Jana Van Fleet's Questions

1. Haley Elliott, Jake's wife, seems very insecure about her looks. Do you think more middle-class women should put self-care as a higher priority? When is the last time you had a spa treatment?

2. Do you think I'm pretty?

3. Jake once told me that I made him feel interesting for the first time in a long time. If I ever try to lure a man away from his marriage again, I think I'll use that technique. Why do you think it's so effective?

Micah's Questions

1. My Spanish teacher went nuts after she had her kid. Do you have kids, and are you nuts? Please explain.

2. Do you like punk fusion with hard rock influences, and, if so, do you have any contacts at a major recording label?

Willow's Questions

1. Heidi and Jake are not the first couple to ignore Solomon's advice: "Keep vigilant watch over your heart;

that's where life starts" (Proverbs 4:23). Have you ever failed to keep watch over your heart and reaped the consequences? What are some practical ways we can guard our hearts?

2. Heidi rips on me for having lived in a commune when I was young. Though I no longer advocate hashish abuse, I do miss the open and giving spirit that was so much a part of my years there. Do you think the church can learn anything from hippies, or am I just romanticizing a time best forgotten?

Nora's Questions (Dictated)

1. My mom is so great. She makes this amazing milkshake four or five times a day, and she keeps me relatively clean, though sometimes she says I stink. Do you ever stink? Do you like milkshakes?

2. My dad and mom usually get along. When they argue, though, I try to distract them by pitching a royal fit. Don't you think this is genius? If you have kids, do they know how to make you stop fighting with your spouse? Do you think I'm too young to know the words "genius" and "spouse"?

micah's songbook

Dazzle Me
A Song for Holly Daze 2005

They say nothing's new under the sun.
I say they haven't met you.
They say the world's tired and done.
I say the world just needs a clue.

CHORUS:
And it's you.
You dazzle, you razzle, you shine.
And it's you.
I just can't get you out of my mind.
Yeah, it's you.
You razzle, you dazzle divine.
Yeah, it's you. Oh, yeah. It's you.

They say that forever's a game.
I say you can change me.
They say love hurts just the same.
I say the pain doesn't scare me.

(Repeat CHORUS three times and fade.)

Rain

It's raining.
You're crying.
You heard what I said.

You've cheated.
You're lying.
But I won't wish you dead.

CHORUS:
And the reason
For this season
Of my kindness to you
Is my big heart
So much bigger
Than you, oh, yeah, you.

(You you you you.)

It's easy
Just so easy
To be true to your love.

But you failed me,
Oh so miserably
And now you want a hug?

(CHORUS)

Coffee Shop

I met her at a coffee shop.
She was so hot, I thought I'd drop.
She came each day
To get her cup of joe.

She met me at the coffee shop.
Said yes to me for just one stop.
She broke my heart
And took the cup of joe.

CHORUS:
But I don't miss her, see?
I wanted to be free.
I must have seen her through a coffee haze.

I'll just forget her, see?
It won't be tough for me
Because my coffee's really what I crave.

willow's pasta of love

1 pound whole-wheat penne
¼ cup extra-virgin olive oil
¼ cup canola oil
½ cup red onion, sliced
½ cup green pepper, sliced
1 cup portobello mushrooms, sliced
Salt and fresh cracked pepper, to taste
1 cup Roma tomatoes, diced
2–3 tablespoons Pesto Sauce (next page)
2 4-oz grilled chicken breasts, sliced, or 12 cooked
  shrimp

Cook pasta in large pot of boiling salted water until tender but still firm to bite, stirring occasionally. Drain. Return pasta to pot.

Heat olive oil and canola oil in large heavy skillet over medium heat. Add onions, peppers, and mushrooms, and sauté until tender. Salt and pepper to taste.

Combine mushroom mixture with pasta. Add Roma tomatoes. Toss to mix and add Pesto Sauce. Add grilled chicken or shrimp before serving. Serves 4.

Pesto Sauce

4 cups fresh basil leaves, well packed

4 cloves garlic, lightly crushed and peeled

1 cup pine nuts or walnuts (or a combination of the two)

1½ cups freshly grated Parmesan cheese

1½ cups extra-virgin olive oil

Salt and pepper to taste

Place basil leaves and garlic in food processor or blender and process until leaves are finely chopped. Add nuts and process until nuts are finely chopped. Add cheese and process until combined. With processor running, add olive oil in a slow, steady stream. After oil is incorporated, turn off processor and salt and pepper to taste.

If not using immediately, store in an airtight container with a thin coating of olive oil on top to keep the sauce from turning dark. Pesto will keep well in the refrigerator for a week or more. This recipe yields approximately 3½ to 4 cups and can be halved.

Recipe courtesy of Chef Robert Lewis
www.happydiabetic.com

An entry from Heidi's diary, three years later . . .

As usual, the dishes are washed, floors are waxed, toilets are sparkling. I'm waiting for someone to dirty their clothes so I have enough laundry for a load. I've frozen enough meals to bring us into 2019, and I've taken up crochet and yodeling as spare-time amusements. My daughter, Nora, is brilliant, has only contradicted me once, and is busy organizing fundraisers for needy children. Such are the direct results of my choice to stay home full-time.

I'd write more in this journal, handmade with paper I pressed from my own dried-flower arrangements, but my soufflé is peaking and my bonbons need chilling.

Ah, the life of a stay-at-home mom.

Um, not exactly.

℮ ℈ ℮

Look for Heidi's latest dose of chaos in stores nationwide, May 2007.

℮ ℈ ℮

author's note/living proof

Everybody has a story. You have been kind enough to read Heidi and Jake's, and, if I may, I'd like to share my own. Though I'm always up for a good work of fiction, what follows is the true account of a pivotal moment in this writer's life. May the mercy I've been shown rain on you as you read.

❧ ❧ ❧

When I was two years old, my head was run over by a big red convertible. This story has been a part of me for twenty-eight years, but I didn't really understand it until I met my daughter. Like most things in my life, the accident became more vibrant, the colors more vivid, and the conclusion more heart-gripping after the birth of my sweet Ana.

❧ ❧ ❧

Late in the summer of 1977, my father challenged the God of the universe to a duel. My dad is into duels. He used to challenge all three of us kids to beat him in tackle football. Or golf. Badminton even. We've tired of his standing invitation to beat him in a swim across the lake. Every Fourth of July, he ignores the groans and coerces the entire extended family into

Randy's Forced Fun Summer Olympics, which include gunny sack races and pie-eating contests. Once, he went so far as to challenge our family friend Joann, who can run the socks off most antelopes, to a half marathon, boasting he wouldn't even need to train for it. His only preparation was to sleep in his running gear the night before the race. Remembrance of this little incident and its painful aftermath still brings a sheepish grin to my dad's face.

When we were little, an Energizer Bunny dad was by far the best you could have. For example, Dad's *joie de vivre* translated into the most insanely fun vacations, which my mother hated. Dad did not believe in lying on a beach when he could be the only middle-aged Midwesterner trying out a boogie board. Why sip iced tea by the pool when he could get his kids to help force its still waters into a man-made typhoon? And did anyone *really* obey those traffic signs at go-kart tracks? These tendencies were cause for alarm for my mother, who was trying to raise calm children. But they were golden to her three kids, who saw their dad as the Iowan Indiana Jones.

Certainly it was this unscratchable itch for action that propelled my young father into the throne room of God in the summer of 1977. Dad had been raised by Christian parents who were involved in their church and encouraged their five children to love God and to love people. My father followed their rules, treated others with respect, and attended their small-town church each Sunday. By the time he'd turned twenty-eight, however, Dad was sick of playing the part. He'd obeyed, and he'd participated in the weekly ritual of worship. He'd married his high school sweetheart and had stood with her five years later for their infant daughter's baptism into the faith. But the reality of God had eluded him. No more faking it, he thought and demanded of God, "If You're real, reveal Yourself to me. Because if not, I have better things to do."

So much for finesse with the Almighty.

My father did receive the burning bush he'd wanted. In fact, he practically had to duck to avoid the flames.

℮ ℈ ℮

My mom is hilarious. All who know her appreciate her self-deprecating, rollicking sense of humor. She has no qualms admitting her skirt fell off one Sunday when praying at the altar in front of the church. She has been known to make her children roll with laughter as she dances in the living room to the Beatles' greatest hits. Once she and I nearly got kicked out of the Christian bookstore, where employees are paid to be extra patient with the riffraff, because we were raising too much of a ruckus by the flannel boards.

It is precisely this sense of humor that has helped preserve my parents' marriage. My mom's ability to laugh kept her from divorcing Dad when, for example, she was unable to park in their garage from 1989 to 2004 (Dad loves Sam's Club and Home Depot more than he loves space in his garage). She has chosen to laugh though her house looks like a used car lot each Christmas when Dad gets carried away with the lights (Sam's Club again). She even laughed through gritted teeth when Dad's efforts at "organizing" resulted in throwing away things like birth certificates, wedding invitations, and, most recently, her cell phone charger.

This is not to say our house was a series of *I Love Lucy* episodes. As my mother now tells it, during the time before my accident, she and Dad did their fair share of hashing things out. My mom, the one who usually lets things roll, was picking a fight. She knew that buying in bulk, decorating in a frenzy, and cleaning with wild abandon were nonissues compared to the spiritual health of our family. While my dad had been going through the motions of unenthusiastic church attendance, my mother was neck-deep in spiritual upheaval. She had begun to know God on a personal level, to experience life-changing grace on a daily basis. She had met others who had a palpable passion for knowing God, and she was hungry for the same.

My dad didn't see the draw. He was not in the same place, and this irked my normally unfazed mother. Dad thought Mom was getting woo-woo on him, and he wasn't too pleased. For her part, Mom knew this was an important battle, and it frustrated her that this fresh, renewing relationship she was growing with God was not first on Dad's priority list.

Enter a two-ton red convertible. God does have a way of getting our attention.

ℰ ◔ ℰ

My daughter, Ana, has blue eyes I could swim in, curls that multiply in humidity, and a personality that is nearly uncontained by her three-year-old frame. She has brightened, broadened, and made my life explode with new love, new patience, and new passion. She has also increased exponentially my desire to move to a remote island where no one can hurt her. I knew we were in trouble early on when the first mosquito that dared land on Ana's head seriously regretted it. I'm shocked by the mother bear instinct that washes over me when Ana's friendly smiles or waves go unacknowledged. The love I have for my daughter is stubborn and ferocious, the same love my parents have held toward me with open hands all my life.

I shiver, then, to imagine the panic that must have gripped my parents that sunny September day nearly thirty years ago. Shortly after Dad's ultimatum prayer, my mom and I were outside playing in our backyard. When my father came home for lunch, Mom went to greet him and left me playing in the sandbox. While my parents talked in the kitchen, I toddled around to the front yard.

Within seconds they heard a soul-wrenching scream from next door. My parents ran out of the house to see our neighbor Kathy, knees buckled on her driveway pavement. She was screaming and crying over my little body, which lay limp under her car. Her convertible's right rear wheel had run over my head. My dad, ignoring all medical knowledge he'd accrued in his dental profession and bypassing the rule to never move the victim of a head injury, picked up his little girl and gave me to my mom. I lay in her lap on the way to the hospital.

I never lost consciousness, but I'd whimper. I'm weeping as I write this just to think of Ana's little frame in my lap. I would have wanted her to scream, cry, carry on. I would have wanted her to be angry with me for my negligence, hit me, or hurt me to even the score. A whimper would have killed me. Too quiet, too resigned, far too vulnerable.

The hospital physicians were not hopeful. By all outward appearances, I had only scrapes and bruises. But the tire had passed over my head, and I had a bilateral skull fracture. We had entered some very scary territory. Possible outcomes ranged from severe brain damage to paralysis to death.

At this point, my mother should have hit the panic button. I'm quite certain that if I had been the young mother in question, you would have found me clinging to the nearest candy striper with a viselike grip. But this is where the proverbial rubber met the road, and my mom was ready. She had sought out God and had found Him to be real, near, and satisfying. When her journey brought her to this unbearably steep cliff, she was able to breathe deeply. Mom has told me since that through this time, others thought she was in shock, so deep was her calm. But she says simply, "I remember thinking, This is what grace feels like."

For his part, my father recognized this to be the end to the duel. Even in the valley of shadows, he did not feel lost. He did not despair. He was able to rest in a peace inexplicable, a mercy that cushioned this startling fall. To this day, three decades later, my father is unable to get through this story without tears because of the way the God of the universe heard and answered his cry.

Even with a peace that defied human understanding, my parents knew the outlook was bleak. But bleak outlooks are the specialty of a great God. Mom and Dad called family, friends, neighborhood churches, and colleagues to ask for their prayers. The number multiplied until thousands were praying. My parents remember a particularly sweet turning point when, after a few days, I looked at them and said, "I want Mommy read me." The doctors could not explain what resulted. After five days in the hospital, without having taken even a Children's Tylenol, I went home with my mom and dad. No scarring. No disfigurement. No brain damage. Only many, many thankful hearts and softened spirits that were changed by God's dramatic, stubborn love.

e ᴐ e

I've heard and told this story all my life. I've grown up reading the yellowed newspaper clippings, fingering the little shirt that's cut right up the center where doctors had to remove it, meeting people who light up when they see me and say, "You're the miracle baby!" I've told this story in two languages and in six countries. But I've come to know that this story is not mine alone.

This is my mother's story. She is the one who learned to lean on everlasting arms when her own legs gave out. She is the one who met the peace of God in a new, tangible way during dark days. She is the mother who was able to forgive herself for a moment's mistake and embrace the freedom of giving hard memories to a merciful God. My mom learned the light, easy yoke of grace and felt the soft rain of God's never-failing, constant presence.

This is my father's story. He is the one for whom God hand-crafted a most precious response to his question. His daughter was the patient of an amazed neurologist who said my recovery was, indeed, the stuff of miracles. God had revealed Himself in a way tailor-made for my nonstop, vibrant, impatient father. Answer in hand, Dad dove into knowing God with the same set jaw and unbridled determination he'd shown in the initial throne room showdown. God had met Dad right where he stood, and my father has pulled our family along on a wild, God-drenched adventure ever since.

And this is my story. This is how I know beyond doubt that all things truly are possible to those who believe. This is my comfort in knowing I can trust my Ana to rest safely in the large, capable hands of a God of grace. This story is the backbone of my belief that though I love Ana so much it hurts, the God who created her loves her even more and will hold her even when I slip. Of this I am living proof.

about the author

KIMBERLY STUART lives with her husband and two children in Iowa, where she writes faithfully before laundry and during nap time. For more information about Kimberly, visit www.kimberlystuart.com.

EXCITING NEW FICTION FROM NAVPRESS.

A Mile from Sunday
Jo Kadlecek   1-60006-028-5

Can a religion reporter find a good story among the church bulletins for barbecues and bingo? One tip can change—or end—a career, as Jonna Lightfoot McLaughlin soon learns.

Murder, Mayhem, and a Fine Man
Claudia Mair Burney   1-57683-978-8

For Amanda Bell Brown, turning forty is murder! How's a woman supposed to grapple with her faith when she finds herself in the middle of mysteries—and not the God kind?

Watching the Tree Limbs
Mary E. DeMuth   1-57683-926-5

Nine-year-old Mara thought life just might be perfect if only she could live in the big white Victorian house. Then she moved in and found she wasn't the only one keeping an ugly secret.

Wishing on Dandelions
Mary E. DeMuth   1-57683-953-2

At seventeen, life for Maranatha hasn't gotten any easier. The abuse has stopped, but she is anything but healed. As young men begin to show interest in her, will she be able to let go of the past and let love in?

Visit your local Christian bookstore,
call NavPress at 1-800-366-7788,
or log on to www.navpress.com to purchase.
To locate a Christian bookstore near you, call 1-800-991-7747.

NAVPRESS
BRINGING TRUTH TO LIFE
www.navpress.com

With her baby on one side and her career on the other, what's a girl to do?

etc.

bonus content includes:
- ▸ reader's guide
- ▸ Micah's songbook
- ▸ sneak preview
- ▸ and more

As maternity leave comes to an end for Heidi Elliott, so does virtually everything she thought she knew. The substitute filling in for her high school Spanish classes has made a complete mess—not just with her students, but perhaps in a way far more personal. Her husband has made a habit of going out of his way to help a beautiful and wealthy client. And now, to further complicate things, Heidi's old boyfriend has moved back into the neighborhood.

Fiercely independent, Heidi has never been one for group activities, much less church chats and teas. Pushed into accepting an invitation to the Wednesday night Moms' Group, she finds herself in a sea of polyester, polka dots, big hair, and surprisingly strong women who just might hold the lifeline she didn't think she needed.

"Heidi Elliott is my new best friend. I loved every hilarious, insightful, grace-drenched word of this novel and hated to see it end!"

CLAUDIA MAIR BURNEY, The Ragamuffin Diva, author of the AMANDA BELL BROWN mystery series

"Smart. Sassy. Superb! Kimberly Stuart has created a flawless and funny novel that will make you wish for more when the last page is turned."

GINGER GARRETT, author of Chosen: The Lost Diaries of Queen Esther and Dark Hour

KIMBERLY STUART attended Wheaton College (Wheaton, Illinois) and St. Olaf College (Northfield, Minnesota). She has taught Spanish, English as a second language, and bilingual education in Chicago, Minneapolis, Costa Rica, and rural Iowa. She currently lives in West Des Moines, Iowa.

USA $12.99

FICTION
CONTEMPORARY
MOM-LIT

ISBN 1-60006-076-5

9 781600 060762

51299

NAVPRESS
BRINGING TRUTH TO LIFE
www.navpress.com